MURDER
IN THE TEA LEAVES

A BLAKE SISTERS TRAVEL MYSTERY – BOOK 2

CARTER FIELDING

Published by Carter Fielding Press
5237 River Road, #304
Bethesda, MD 20216

Editing, Design, and Production by Bublish, Inc.
ISBN: 978-1-64704-494-7 (eBook)
ISBN: 978-1-64704-495-4 (Paperback)

**For information about the author and her projects
please visit:
www.mcarterfielding.com**

To Mommy and Daddy—
Thanks for never clipping my wings!

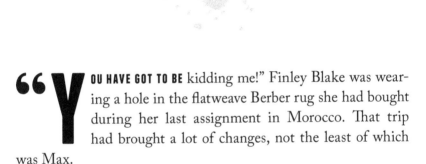

1

"**Y**OU HAVE GOT TO BE kidding me!" Finley Blake was wearing a hole in the flatweave Berber rug she had bought during her last assignment in Morocco. That trip had brought a lot of changes, not the least of which was Max.

"You just had me book my flight. Last night, in fact!" Her voice reflected the agitation she felt. Her shoulders were creeping up to her ears. Her jaw was moving back and forth—a sure sign she was upset. "So where am I off to now?"

Finley was back home in Manhattan, talking to Dan Burton, her editor at *Traveler's Tales*, a high-end travel magazine that had been giving her freelance work for the past several months, ever since her first "48 Hours in…" article. That article focused on the exotic wonders of Casablanca, complete with descriptions of all the best food, shopping, and historical sights that could be absorbed in two days.

The success of the Casablanca article, and the eye-catching photos that had accompanied it, ensured that work would be steady for a few months. Dan kept printing her stories, both the short "48 Hours" pieces that she had done on Fes, Barcelona, and Tangier, as well as some more in-depth reporting on Sienna, Dubrovnik, and Bruges that she had done just a couple of months ago.

Truth be told, Dan was more than her boss. He was also her friend—he had been, in fact, since their early law school days. They often used to sit together in class because of their last names, Blake and Burton, and had remained friends over the years. They both also abandoned the law long ago and took up other careers: Finley in consulting and Dan in journalism. When Finley decided to leave the consulting firm where she was a senior partner, Dan was the first person she called.

Dan had brought her on *Traveler's Tales* provisionally at first, but the sales-worthiness of her stories and photos earned her a regular slot. Dan would have loved to hire her on the permanent staff, but Finley wanted the freedom to pick and choose which assignments she took. And that was what had her so riled now.

The original assignment she had opted for would have taken her to India for a piece on preserving the cultural heritage of tribal peoples from Bihar, Jharkhand, and Odisha. Finley would get to see Max, who was now in Delhi. Their relationship was a complicated one that had started years ago during an earlier stint in Morocco. It was interrupted for almost three years after that because of a profound misunderstanding that had nearly broken them both.

"If we hadn't reviewed the assignment and all the travel logistics just yesterday, I wouldn't be having this reaction," Finley continued. "But I literally booked the flight, hotel, and driver last night because I thought everything was a go." Finley knew that this was only a half-truth. *He doesn't have to know the real reason I'm pissed. I told Max I was coming. I really want to see him.*

"I know, but I have a new staff writer coming on, and we're shifting the focus to Delhi, which is an easier story. We'll hold off on your story for another issue." Dan could hear the frustration in Finley's voice. And while she didn't talk about her personal life much, he had seen how devastated she was four years ago when she returned to New York. How she had thrown herself into her work to fill the void created by the loss of something precious.

Dan had met Max socially before, when all three of them used to work in Manhattan. He knew then that Finley and Max had been close in Tangier all those years ago and that something had happened, but he never found out what had caused her to come home so broken. What he did know was that when she returned from Morocco this time, some eight months ago, whatever hurt there had been was healed and she readily spoke Max's name.

"I need a more experienced writer on this story, and I think you'll do it justice."

"Don't start buttering me up," Finley's voice was tight, but she masked a smile. "You know I can still refuse it and sit this one out."

"I don't think you're going to want to, though." Dan could tell she was warming up to the new potential location, even without knowing where it was. "It's politically complex, and you'll know how to balance the perspectives and still get travelers to want to go."

"You going to tell me where it is or just keep me guessing?"

"You want to guess?"

"No, just tell me so I can say no."

"You'd say no to Sri Lanka? As I recall, you called it 'paradise on earth.'"

Finley was quiet. As much as she wanted to say no, she knew Dan had her trapped. She sighed and then let out a small laugh.

"I give up. You got me," she said. "I can't say no. When do I leave?"

Dan explained the Colombo focus of the assignment and reviewed the logistics.

"I managed to swing a bit of budget. But—" Dan started.

"—don't expect it every time," Finley finished. Dan always said that, but still managed to find money to fund her assignments. She wasn't hurting for money. The buyout from the consulting firm was generous and positioned her well for the future. Still, why pay for things out of pocket when someone else was willing to cover the cost up-front?

It was still midafternoon when she hung up with Dan. She was dreading the call to Max, so she put it off. The less she thought about it, the less she would be filled with that longing for Max that she had been suppressing for months now.

Once, she saw Max in New York for two weeks. He had arranged to meet a potential client there instead of in London so that they could spend some time together. Besides that, there was one long weekend in Barcelona when she was working on a story about the rise of tango bars in the city. She and Max took a class and danced a *tanda* or two at Centro Gallego de Barcelona, never progressing to the faster-paced *milagro*. That was almost two months ago.

Instead of calling Max, she speed-dialed her sister, S. Whittaker Blake, known to all as simply "Whitt." *Or Half-Whitt. I haven't called her that in years.* Whitt lived in Manila most of the time, but because she worked for a development bank, she was on the road more often than not. Finley and Whitt saw each other a couple of times a year back in the US when Whitt had home leave. In between, they tried to work their travel schedules so that they could meet somewhere equidistant to wherever they were working. Morocco was a bit out of the way for Whitt last time, who had been on her way to meetings in Tbilisi, but it proved to be a worthwhile trip in so many ways.

"Hello? Whitt Blake," Whitt had her work voice on today.

Finley laughed. Her little sister was all grown up. Whitt was almost six years younger and had settled into her career as a Young Professional at the bank. She was also settling into a relationship with an incredibly handsome young entrepreneur named David, who was building export relationships with wine and walnut vendors in Georgia.

Whitt had met David a year ago through mutual friends in Tbilisi, and they had been together ever since. He had had a hand in Finley and Whitt's adventures in Morocco—and he stuck around to see how things with Whitt might play out. Finley had to give him credit. He was made of stronger stuff than what she had imagined when Whitt first started talking about him.

"Hey, what are you up to?"

"Not much. Just doing revenue projections for that same microfinance project that I've been working on for months." She tried to sound frustrated that the project was taking so long to get structured, but Finley knew she was glad to be in Tbilisi as long as David was there. "When do you leave for Delhi?"

"I don't," Finley said and heard her sister take in a breath. *She's probably waiting for curses or tears. Let's see how long she holds her breath waiting for me to start screaming.* Finley waited.

She stared at the early rush-hour traffic that was building up on Amsterdam. The double-paned windows muffled the honking and noise of an impatient city. Pedestrians wove in and out of the stopped cars, taking advantage of the suspended animation to hurry home and take their kids to ballet—or to make it to a nail appointment. *Welcome to New York.*

Whitt chose her words carefully. "Is your trip delayed?"

"No, canceled. The assignment was given to a new writer," Finley looked away from the window and paused.

Whitt was quiet. The silence was heavy. Finley could imagine Whitt's brow furrowing, and her hand moving slowly to release the mouse and pick up her ginger tea from the mini warming plate. *I should put her out of her misery. She's thinking too much. Her brain is going to explode trying to figure out what to say that won't put me in tears.*

Finley continued, "I got Sri Lanka, instead. Mainly Colombo."

"So you can still see each other," Whitt exhaled finally and smiled to herself. *She has been missing him so much. Max has probably been going through the same struggle. They are such a confusing couple.*

"Yeah, but I haven't told him about the change of plans yet. I'll deal with it tonight." Finley would catch him before he headed to work—Delhi time—just after his run.

"As long as you can see each other, he'll be fine. And Colombo is just a short flight from Delhi."

"How's David?" Finley suddenly wondered if he was sitting right there. He might be if she was working from home. "When do I get to see you guys?"

"He's fine. In a meeting downtown," Whitt said. "I was wondering—when you said Colombo—if you wanted to exchange the trip to Uzbekistan for more time in Sri Lanka."

Whitt had given Finley a trip to Central Asia for her thirtieth birthday that she still hadn't redeemed. Finley loved her sister's taste in gifts: either really expensive pieces of jewelry or trips to faraway places. She loved both, so the surprise was always there no matter what Whitt chose. "We didn't have time to explore Galle or much of the south last trip," she continued.

"Can you get away on such short notice?" Finley asked. "I know you must have the time saved up, as hard as you work."

"I think I can. Just one small hurdle in the numbers."

"David coming too?"

"Nope, I'll leave him here," Whitt said lightly. "You know, absence makes the heart grow fonder and all that."

Finley tensed. *That doesn't sound good. Wonder what's up? She's making a joke of it, but I don't think it's intended to be funny.* Her sister played the tough cookie as her public persona, but she was a softie who was pretty closed with her emotions. She could be bleeding inside and still make some cavalier comment to deflect the pain. You never could tell for sure. *Maybe it is time for some girl talk.*

"Sure. Let me get this story out of the way, and then we can have some fun."

"Where do you want to go?"

"Surprise me. Only request is that we do Yala again."

Whitt had planned the last trip to Sri Lanka, even though it was Finley's graduation gift to her. There had been so many places that Whitt had wanted to see in the northern and central parts of the country that Yala was the only concession they made to go south. They started in Colombo, and then headed to Kandy to see the Temple of the Tooth shrine, before heading to Dambulla to wander the Buddha caves and to take a quick tour of Anuradhapura.

They hadn't gone further north to Jaffna due to reports of political unrest. Instead, they headed southwest to Polonnaruwa, an ancient city dating back thousands of years, with a quick stop in Sigiriya to climb Lion's Mountain. The panoramic view from the top of the 200-foot outcropping—which had purportedly served as both an old monastery and a palace—was surreal. Whitt said she could imagine a king looking out on this vista every morning, knowing that all that his eye could see was his kingdom. They ended that trip leopard spotting in Yala.

"Galle OK as our launch point?" Whitt asked. "Great gem shopping."

Finley smiled to herself. Whitt always had a nose for the best shopping in town, and this trip would be no different. Without David there to carry packages, Finley knew she would serve the role of Sherpa. Thank goodness that gems were small and light!

"Works for me. Got to go. Another call coming in, but I'll talk to you soon. Love you."

"Me too," was all she heard as the call dropped, and Mooney's face appeared on her screen. Mooney Allen was one of her dearest friends. They met in New York after Finley had returned from Tangier the first time. Mooney had been a lifeline back during that time and remained a trusted confidant.

"Don't forget drinks tonight."

Finley screwed up her face and cursed under her breath. Mooney made it her job to ensure all her friends got out and enjoyed the fabulous happenings in the city. She was especially mindful of Finley's tendency to pull on her sweats, order in Thai or Lebanese food, and curl up with a book for days on end.

Mooney knew about Max and wanted to help Finley figure out what she wanted from that relationship, but she also hated for Finley to waste opportunities and miss seeing "what else was out there," as she was fond of saying. In particular, Mooney wanted Finley to at least consider Logan Reynolds, a slightly older, very successful entrepreneur, who was attractive, rich, and above all, "FOF"—fond of Finley.

"You forgot," Mooney continued reproachfully. "That's why I called. In fact, I'll come pick you up in forty-five minutes."

Before Finley could protest, Mooney had clicked off. Finley sat looking at the phone. She stuck out her tongue at Mooney's picture before it faded and then put down her phone. *I don't want to go out. I don't have anything to wear.* She was glad she hadn't tried that excuse on Mooney. Mooney would have simply swooped in thirty minutes early and torn Finley's closet apart putting together killer outfits for the night.

Finley moved to the closet to see what she could piece together for drinks. She didn't feel like getting dressed up, but if she didn't make an effort, she would have to deal with Mooney's mouth all weekend and into next week. And she wanted—needed—to focus on getting ready for Colombo, scoping out ideas and angles for a story, and figuring out what to take. Mooney might be useful with that.

By the time Mooney arrived, Finley had rummaged the closet for an outfit and turned up with only a pair of black skinny jeans, a black cashmere turtleneck, and some dressy black boots. Granted the boots were Jimmy Choo's from three seasons ago, but she had to admit that she could just as easily have gone grocery shopping at Dag's as gone to drinks at Cork in this. She grabbed a pair of large Berber earrings and some bangles when the doorbell rang.

"I'm trying to decide whether I like it or not." Mooney had stepped in and then held Finley at arm's length to determine whether she approved of what she was wearing.

"I haven't done my hair yet." Finley pulled at the hair tie that was holding her mass of curls back. She had kept it pixie short for almost four years but was now letting it slowly grow out. It wasn't to her waist as it had been years ago, but it had grown down to her shoulders and was thick and heavy.

She headed to the bathroom and finished her makeup before she started detangling her curls with her fingers. The hair around her temples and brow fell into soft tendrils that framed her face. She added a bit more blush to meet the delicate wisps that played close to her dark green eyes and then added a pop of brick-red matte lipstick to break up the blackness of her clothes.

"You know, I love that on you." Mooney was standing at the bathroom door, watching as Finley put the final touches on her makeup. "It isn't me, but it is so understatedly you."

The contrast between them was indeed marked. Finley in her black-on-black outfit, alligator-green eyes and matte-red lips—the only flashes of color—and Mooney, all brightness and light with her ash-blond tresses catching the beams from the hall and reflecting it back in her crystalline-blue eyes. Finley smiled at their yin-yang looks. She grabbed her long Kashmiri-embroidered duster, cut the lights, and they were out of the door.

Cork was surprisingly quiet for a Friday night. Mooney had called ahead to reserve their usual high-bar table toward the front window, but she really didn't need to, given the slow crowd that was there. It might have been the cold dampness in the air. It was February after all. *Goodness, I will be glad for Colombo's warm weather. Humidity, I can take. Anything but this cold.*

Their table was starting to fill with friends from Mooney's work, as well as Finley's former consulting firm. Even though many had left to go to other positions in the city, they had stayed tight friends and looked forward to catching up over drinks each week with people that knew them well enough to just enjoy their company without judgment. Finley valued that when she had come back from Tangier the first time, licking her wounds.

"Love those earrings!" Lydia, Mooney's roommate and Finley's former classmate from law school, was reaching over the narrow table to hold the thick pendant dangles to the light. "Where'd you get them? And don't tell me some place exotic!"

Finley reached up to touch the etching on the earrings, trying to remember where and when she had gotten them. When her fingers traced the intricate hammer work on them, she smiled, remembering well that they had come from Max and had been a gift from this last trip in Fes. Whitt and David had left by that point, and Max accompanied Finley to Fes for her final segment of the Moroccan assignment. He had purchased them there without her knowing and then presented them to her as she was getting on the plane in Tangier to head home.

"Don't open this until you're in the air," he had said, pressing a small woven bag into her hand as she stepped toward security.

She was well into the second hour of the flight before she loosened the black cord on the brocade pouch and unwrapped the earrings. They matched the silver beadwork on a necklace he had given her years ago, when they first met. The Berber symbols etched on both signified endless time.

"In Morocco," was all she said.

"Speaking of Morocco, I still owe you dinner." Someone had come up behind her, slipped an arm around her waist and kissed her cheek. It was Logan. "When you left for Morocco last year, I promised you a raincheck for dinner, and you haven't called it in yet."

Mooney watched Finley's face to see how she was going to get out of this one. Finley and Logan had been out several times before Finley and Max reconnected. And they had continued to hang out together over drinks, like tonight. But Finley had put off his recent attempts to get her alone, especially over an intimate dinner. As much as she liked him as a friend, even if there had been no Max, she probably wouldn't have seriously dated him. But now, there was a Max.

"You do indeed," Finley acknowledged. She was going to have to handle this carefully since he was one of Mooney's clients.

Finley was saved from having to further commit by a former colleague who called her over to look at pictures of her baby. By the time she returned to her stool, everyone was deciding where to go for dinner. They settled on Rocco's, a steakhouse in the Flatiron District, and the group began piling into cabs for the short trip downtown. As fate would have it, Logan put Finley into a cab and then hopped in beside her.

"So where do you want to use your raincheck? The world is your oyster," Logan said as the cab entered the long line of traffic heading south on Fifth. "You name the place. Just the two of us. Anywhere in the world."

Finley knew that he meant it. If she had said she wanted steak *frites* in a Paris bistro in Saint-Germain-des-Prés—or even sushi in Ginza, Tokyo—Logan would have scheduled his plane and whisked her off for dinner in France or Japan, even if it was one that she could easily have gotten in New York. She smiled at the privileges that wealth could bring.

"I'm going to have to think on that for a while," Finley said. "I leave in a few days on another assignment, so I'll have a couple of long plane rides to contemplate where I want to go."

"You're leaving me again? Where to now?"

"Colombo for a couple of weeks. And then further south with my sister."

Logan turned to face her, smiling slightly. "Any other guy would think that you're trying to avoid me." He paused. "Are you?"

Finley returned his look and answered honestly. There was no point in not being direct and truthful. "No, I like your company. You're an exceedingly interesting man, but I think we both know that I'm not interested in you."

She straightened in her seat, turning her gaze forward and matching her smile to his. "And if you were truly honest, you would concede that it isn't me that you want. It's the chase you like, not the catch!"

Logan opened his mouth to speak, shut it, sighed, and then burst into laughter. "You got me! Until you said it, I don't think I realized it myself. Touché!"

He lifted her gloved hand from her lap and held it in his. Theirs was going to be a long and complex friendship. The stuff of legends. They continued the rest of the trip in companionable silence. The cabbie glanced in his mirror a few times, shook his head, and turned up the radio.

2

MAX TURNED OUT TO BE understanding about the shift in story assignment to Sri Lanka. He immediately booked a flight to see her for a few days in Colombo shortly after her arrival. He had never been to Sri Lanka and was looking forward to having her show him around. Unlike Morocco, of which he had deep knowledge, the trip to Colombo would be a mini adventure. And the tightness in his voice suggested that he needed a break.

"How's the story going?" Max had called her on FaceTime and was watching as she grabbed her wine and moved to the veranda. He could hear the waves crashing on the rocks below. "Flip the camera so I can see the water."

Finley turned her iPad toward the ocean. She had used her *Traveler's Tales* discount to book an ocean view room at the Galle Face Hotel—a quintessential landmark in Colombo. The sea behind the hotel was angry today, lashing the rocks upon which the hotel sat and spraying the grass terrace with washes of salty mist. She had to raise her voice to be heard above the din.

"Pretty, isn't it? Last night, the water was much quieter." Finley had moved the camera so he could see her face. "I had a drink and dinner on the terrace. Very old-world."

She continued, tracing the contours of his face on the screen with her eyes, trying to iron out the worry that creased his brow. "The story is shaping up. I did some interviews yesterday with travel agents and the Ministry of Tourism, and then I did a tuk-tuk tour to get my bearings. Heading to the temple later today."

She was talking about Gangaramaya Vihara, a historic Buddhist temple built in the late 1800s when Sri Lanka was under British colonial rule. The intricately decorated building and its grounds housed several large Buddhas that were revered by practitioners, including an array of Buddhas on stacked platforms that conjured the South Asian influences of the stupas at Borobudur in Indonesia.

"How about you? When do the surveys launch?" she asked.

He had been working on this project for the past three months and was likely to remain in Delhi for at least the next year. The effort was going well, but he wondered about the ultimate impact.

"Things are heating up now. We head out to the field to canvass next week," he said. "Asking rural customers about the type of healthcare they need when they are used to having none is something of a joke. But we have to start somewhere."

He shifted in his chair, "If the pilot goes well, and we get the kind of data that we hope, we'll roll out across India in the next several months. I may never leave!"

She wanted to give him assurances beyond platitudes, but she knew the pitfalls of wading into large-scale global projects that had the potential to change the world. In reality, these projects sometimes only moved the needle for a random few. Instead of saying anything, though, she waited, listening to the heaviness of his breath as he sighed.

"But I get to see you in a few days, so all is good with the world," he said, locking eyes with her across the screen. His voice softened. "I miss you."

She wanted to get lost in those indescribably delicious teal eyes, to touch the laugh lines around his mouth, to kiss him fully on his perfectly bowed lips. "Miss you, too."

"When do you get in?" Finley continued, exhaling quietly to release some of her pent-up tension.

"Day after tomorrow. In the evening. I'll just arrange a car since it will be late. Unless cabs are available."

"You should be able grab a cab, but I'll arrange a car through the hotel, so you don't have to worry about it. You've got enough on your plate."

"Great. Thanks. Got to go. See you in a couple days." He kissed his finger and put it to the screen. She did the same and held it there until his image turned to black. "Love you."

Finley threw herself into setting up the remaining interviews for her story and scouting out possible locations for photo sessions in the two days leading up to Max's visit. It had taken her a while to get to know the city, but the tuk-tuk tour had helped her place buildings and sites in a mental map, which allowed her to navigate the streets more easily. In just one week, she had visited the Old Parliament Building, Seema Makala, the Bawa-designed Buddhist temple pods in the middle of Beira Lake, Kapikaawatha Shiva Temple—the oldest in Colombo—and Pettah Market, the largest open-air market in the city, in addition to some of the majestic homes around Cinnamon Gardens.

She spent the afternoon after their call taking pictures of the temple and the National Museum, which offered one of the largest collections of artifacts from the ancient dynasties of Kandyan kings. The day was bright and so the sun cast long shadows across the green as Finley walked around the majestic Italianate buildings. She couldn't wait to share with Max the beauty of the city and the richness of the island's history.

When she got back to the hotel, there was a telegram waiting for her. Her heart sank. She drew in her breath before opening it. Telegrams always carried bad news, especially in the era of text and email. Her mind first went to Mama and Daddy, and then to Whitt. The Delhi outgoing caught her eye, and she leaned on the counter as her finger ran along the side of the envelope. *God, make him be all right.*

She pulled open the envelope and ran her eyes over the text, searching for the bad news. She almost laughed out loud when she read the message: *Cancel car. Couldn't wait. Get in tomorrow at two ten. Will grab cab. Kick that other guy out of your bed. You're mine! Love you, MM*

She tucked the message into her backpack, smiled shyly at the bellman who escorted her to the elevator, and then turned to take the stairs up to the fourth floor. She was winded when she reached the top of the stairs. She paused on the landing and touched her bag, just over the place where she had put Max's message for safekeeping. Mad Max, Whitt's and her name for Max, was coming early.

She spent the next morning at the Independence Memorial Hall, an interesting monument that, while pretty, was off the main tourist path. She needed the pictures for her article but wasn't sure that it was something that Max would want to see in the short time he had in the city. She hurried back to the hotel all hot, sweaty, and grungy from the tuk-tuk that she had taken through town and hopped in the shower. She wasn't expecting him for another hour, so when the bell rang, she thought it was the bellhop.

"Yes?" She quickly wrapped a towel around her body and peeked through the peephole.

"Flowers for Madam Blake." The person was standing slightly to the side.

"Can you put them by the door? I'll grab them in a bit."

"You need to sign, madam." She thought she heard a snicker.

"Hold on then." She ran and grabbed a robe and some undies, pulling the robe tie tightly as she headed back to the door. As she began to open it, the person on the other side leaned against the door, throwing her a bit off-balance, and stepped across the threshold.

Finley started to protest when Max wrapped his arms around her and kissed so thoroughly that she began to feel light-headed.

"Do you open your door for any stranger?" he murmured when they came up for air. His hand was playing with the mass of wavy curls that had slipped out of the messy bun she had done for the shower.

"Only if they come bearing flowers." She playfully looked behind his back. "Where are my flowers?"

"I'll have to get you some later. Right now, I need a proper greeting. That one was too short." He proceeded to bury his head in her neck, kissing her shoulders, before working his way up her chin to her lips. Teasingly, he skipped to her nose and forehead before returning to kiss her fully.

"What are you doing here so early?" she asked.

"What? Have you got some other guy warming my place?" His look completely disarmed her.

"No, but if you had come any earlier, I wouldn't have heard you from the shower."

"My loss. I'm sure the front desk would have let me in and then I could have really surprised you."

"How did you get up anyway? I told them that you were coming, but I expected them to ring."

"I told them I was your husband and wanted to surprise you," he smiled sheepishly and led her further into the room. "We can still pretend."

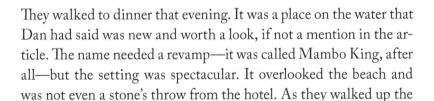

They walked to dinner that evening. It was a place on the water that Dan had said was new and worth a look, if not a mention in the article. The name needed a revamp—it was called Mambo King, after all—but the setting was spectacular. It overlooked the beach and was not even a stone's throw from the hotel. As they walked up the beach to the restaurant, they caught the tail end of the sunset, a fiery, orange ball that suddenly dipped and was snuffed out by the sea.

"What's the plan for tomorrow?" Max asked, after they were seated and had ordered wine. They were slowly looking over the menu, trying to decide if they were hungry enough for a full meal or simply wanted to graze on appetizers. Max entwined his fingers around Finley's as they sat. *If you had asked me a year ago, if I would ever see her again, I would have probably said no. And yet, here we sit. As if the past never happened.*

"What do you want to see? We can do a tuk-tuk tour or we can walk around the old fort. You tell me what you are up for," Finley said. She really didn't care if they stayed in all day. It would be a pity for him to miss the great sights of Colombo, but she wouldn't miss them at all. *Mama would be mortified by my behavior. But Mama didn't have three years to make up for.*

"You. I don't really care what parts of the city we see as long as I get to see them with you." He looked at her so intently that she had to look away. When she met his eyes again, he smiled, "Am I scaring you?"

She had to be honest. "A little. I missed you."

He kissed her fingers and reached to touch her hair. She had left it down in soft, dark waves that hung heavy on her shoulders. She looked like a Mediterranean goddess who had emerged from the sea. It took a few seconds for him to rejoin the conversation.

"If you don't have any place you have to go, let's just play it by ear," he said. "We can wander around. I like seeing you work, so I'll just shadow you."

They sat side by side at dinner, sharing a bottle of wine and plates of fried calamari, chicken tacos, and fried dhal—a global mix of foods that weren't necessarily Sri Lankan, but were what their tongues were calling for. They caught up on the latest news about mutual friends, news that they rarely used their precious time on calls to talk about. They discussed politics, movies they had seen on planes or on Netflix, what kind of dog they would get if they ever stopped traveling. They laughed at silly things they had seen or off-color jokes they had heard. All the normal things they would share if they were together more.

"What would you say if I took a year off and traveled with you?" Max said. The look on his face suggested that he had just blurted out a deep, dark secret that he had been harboring for a very long time. One that he hadn't even admitted to himself.

Finley looked over the rim of her wine glass, biting the inside of her lip, her brows slightly furrowed. "Where did that come from? You're not even halfway through your project. Are you that frustrated with it?"

She continued. Her voice was soft. Her eyes never left his face, which he had turned to stare out at the water. "I'd love to have you with me, finding stories, taking pictures. But I want to be sure you wouldn't be bored. Can you help me understand what you're thinking?"

Max sighed and said, "I just don't want to be without you anymore. I don't want you to be alone. It scares me and makes me sad." He turned and half-laughed. "To be honest, I'm tired of missing you."

"Me too," was the best that Finley could manage. She had neither felt so loved nor been so scared. She sensed that Max was also wading into unknown territory. "We'll figure it out."

Max smiled and squeezed her hand. "You up for dessert?"

While Max ate his chocolate lava cake, Finley outlined Whitt's planned itinerary for the next few weeks. They had missed much of the south last time, and so, this time, they were heading to the city of Galle with a few pit stops. At the last minute, Finley had asked Whitt to book some time in the highlands. The heat, noise, and grit of Colombo had her dreaming of leisurely days in the mists of the tea fields. Besides the highlands, Galle, and Yala, she didn't have any idea what else Whitt had planned. She was looking forward to the surprise.

The next few days with Max flew by. They walked and rode tuk-tuks to almost every inch of Colombo. Finley took him to most of the major sites, including Kelaniya Raja Maha Vihara to see the bodhi tree that is a direct descendant of the one where Lord Buddha attained enlightenment, as well as Number 11, a house designed by Sri Lanka's preeminent architect and creator of so-called "tropical modern" design, Geoffrey Bawa.

They also had a local guide to take them to the best street foods in the city to try *kottu* (mixed grill of spiced shredded meat, vegetables, eggs, and roti), fried chickpeas (spiced with mustard seeds, cumin, and curry leaves), and *pani pol* (a rolled pancake stuffed with ground coconut and treacle). Max had taken her on a similar tour in Fes, exposing her to some of the most sublimely delicious foods she had ever tasted. In addition to wanting to include street food in her article, Finley wanted to experience all the flavors with Max.

In between, they talked about ways for them to be together. If Max was to see this project through, it would be another four or five months before he could break away to join Finley. They batted around options, including Finley going to India after Sri Lanka to work on the tribal story as a true freelancer, without any support from *Traveler's Tales*. And this was where they left it when Max boarded his flight back to Delhi.

Finley sat in the cool, marbled lobby waiting for her sister and looking from the front door to the oceanfront skyline behind her. Whitt's flight from Tbilisi had arrived in Colombo at 3:10 p.m. If traffic delays didn't foil the timetable, Whitt would make it to the hotel just in time for sunset. Finley had just shifted to look at the sky across the grass terrace when she heard footsteps. She turned to see a tall, young, board-thin woman in her signature black crop pants, crisp-white button-down, and Kate Spade flats. She was carrying her every-present black tote bag and a weathered leather duffle.

Though close sisters, physically Finley and Whitt were polar opposites. Both were tall, but where Whitt was that swimmer-straight physique, Finley was slim with curves. Where Whitt was classically pretty with delicate features, Finley had an aquiline nose and full perma-pink lips—an odd combination. Both had green eyes, but Whitt's took after Daddy's unnervingly clear green ones. Finley's were a dark alligator-green like none ever seen before. Whitt's hair was lighter than Finley's chocolate tresses, and where Finley had a mass of heavy waves when her hair got long, Whitt's was shoulder-length and straight.

"Drop your bag at the desk and follow me." Finley said, getting up quickly and grabbing her sister's hand, almost dragging her outside.

"Hello to you, too!"

"I can say hello to you once we get outside."

Finley was walking quickly through the arched passageway that ran from the lobby to the outdoor terrace bar. When she descended the stairs, she stopped, right in the middle of the walkway. The view of the vibrant sunset was framed by two large coconut palms, one on each side, and grounded by matching terra-cotta urns. It was picture-perfect. Finley whipped out her camera and took a shot, and then backed up to put her sister in the frame, backlit by the burnished rays of the sun.

"Now, I can say hello. Hello, how was your flight?" Finley kissed her sister on both cheeks and then gave her a big hug. "You hungry or just want a drink?"

"Drink right now and food later." The two headed toward a table the bartender had pointed to. They turned their chairs toward the sun and sat silently soaking in the last rays of warmth before it sank into the sea.

"So, how was the trip down? It's not that long of a flight, is it?" Finley asked.

"No, relatively speaking, it was short—only nine hours with the layover in Dubai." Whitt laughed. "To folks back in the States, that's a long haul. But when you look at twenty-four to twenty-five hours in the air as a normal flight, this one was short."

"It's all relative. How's Tbilisi Boy?" That was Finley's name for David, Whitt's boyfriend. That she hadn't brought him, coupled with comments Whitt had made here and there, suggested that not all was rosy in Wonderland.

"He's fine. Actually, making some contacts in Moldova for wine distribution."

David owned a distribution business that focused on premium wines, as well as olives, nuts, and their oils. He concentrated on those from the Caucasus, a region where he had family connections on his mother's side. Her family had owned vineyards, and still did. It was through these connections that he had started to penetrate the Georgian, Turkish, and Armenian markets. Now, he was making contacts across the Black Sea in Moldova. He didn't discriminate among the "ancient" wine countries, each of whom claimed to have created winemaking.

"Too bad he couldn't join us." Finley said. She waited, her face placid even as her mind roiled with questions.

Whitt took a sip of the gin and tonic that the waiter had placed in front of her. "Yeah, but I needed some time away."

She sat taking in the quiet night. The angry waves of last week had been replaced by gentle lapping of the water against the rocky cliffs. "So, you want to hear your itinerary?"

Whitt reached into her bag and pulled out a moleskin folder. She unfolded a spreadsheet that looked like next year's revenue projections, with a web of annotations and red marks. Finley leaned in to catch the light of the candle on the text.

"We start in Kandy so you can go to Polonnaruwa again. And then we take the train to Nuwara Eliya. You said that you had always wanted to do that, so this time you get to." The train to Nuwara Eliya ran through some of the most beautiful highland country in the world, complete with waterfalls and high-trestle bridges. Next to the Orient Express, the Kandy-Nuwara Eliya train had always been on Finley's bucket list.

"Then we head to Galle, with a stop in Udawalawe to see the elephants. You're going to get a lot of elephants, to tell the truth." She continued. "We're going to stop at the orphanage on the way to Kandy and then do the safari on the way to Galle."

She paused to signal the waiter for another G&T. When he came with the next round of drinks, Finley ordered some *ulundu vadai*, a dhal fritter with onion and fennel, and Sri Lanka's version of a samosa, a crispy pastry with a spiced-potato filling.

"OK, so from Galle we can do all sorts of day trips, including one to Yala, so you can get more pictures of the leopards."

"And the sloth bears. They're so cute." Finley remembered the last trip to Sri Lanka. It was a year or so after she had come back from Tangier. She had just made partner and to celebrate that, and Whitt's graduation from grad school, they had come to Sri Lanka and the Maldives. "When do we leave?"

"Tomorrow morning. Early!" Whitt said.

"Too early for you to even make a swing by Paradise Road?" Paradise Road was a trendy home-goods store that both Whitt and Finley fell in love with during the last trip. The fact that Whitt, an inveterate acquirer like Mama, had put off shopping was telling—and a bit troubling.

Whitt's gaze faded slightly before she looked out to the water and said, "It can wait."

23

3

BY THE TIME THEY REACHED Kandy, Whitt and Finley had laughed themselves into a fit of tears, and thoughts of trouble-in-paradise between Whitt and David had faded. The comedy of errors that had them giggling hysterically had started at breakfast. As usual, Finley was up, packed, dressed, and waiting with her bag by the door at the ungodly seven thirty departure time that Whitt had dictated in her stern warnings about punctuality the night before. Whitt, on the other hand, was struggling. She had debated between a couple of outfits, settled on one, and promptly spilled her egg hopper down the front of the one she had picked.

The driver, a welcoming fellow by the name of Adesh, had nonetheless gotten the sisters to Pinnawala by ten thirty so they could witness the parade of elephants that passed by each morning as they walked from the orphanage grounds through the streets to the river for their daily bath. The trainers, or *kurawanayakas*, played in the water with elephants of all sizes and scrubbed the animals down, providing delightful displays for shutter-happy tourists.

Finley and Whitt had decided to avoid the crowds along the street and head down to the tiered terraces that banked the river. As Finley finished snapping a shot of a baby elephant balancing on a rock in the middle of the river, one of the larger elephants closer to shore decided to spray the onlookers. Finley, Whitt, and several other tourists found themselves drenched. *Who knew that trunk could hold that much water? Glad it was us and not Mama. She would have made us go to the hotel immediately to get cleaned up.*

Dried and somewhat cleaned, Finley and Whitt spent the next hour in the car reading about the Temple of the Sacred Tooth, a holy place in Kandy where the tooth of the Buddha is believed to be located. The site had political significance as well since it was believed that whoever held the tooth had the right to rule, and Kandy was the last capital of the Sri Lankan kings. When they arrived at the site, Finley and Whitt wandered the grounds, taking in the historical and cultural significance of the palace pavilions and shrines that surrounded the lake.

About two hours later, Whitt and Finley returned to the car, steeped in ancient Sri Lankan history—and ravenous. Adesh suggested Helga's Folly for lunch. While a bit touristy, the kitschy restaurant was a must-see, according to all the guidebooks at least, and it was on the way to the hotel.

Helga's was everything the reviewers claimed and more. The garishly bright colors, surreal wall and ceiling murals, and whimsical decor—like the skeleton on a settee in the front lobby—set the tone for a memorable lunch.

Finley ordered a bottle of chenin blanc before they even fully sat down. The setting seemed perfect to review the craziness of the morning. She sat, sipping her wine and scrolling through her cuts of the day's events.

In addition to the shot of the baby elephant on the rock, she had serendipitously caught the sunlight reflecting through a water spray as an elephant swung his trunk over his head. The play of light refracting through the droplets splattered the frame with tiny rainbows of color on an otherwise gray canvas. She smiled in quiet triumph. *One day, I am going to catch that once-in-a-lifetime shot that will convince me that this is not a hobby but a craft. One day.*

"What are you smiling at?" Whitt had looked up from her guidebook and was studying her sister's face.

Finley leaned over to show her the shot. Whitt's mouth opened slightly in surprise before a look of awe overtook her. "You're good. You're really good."

Maybe that day will be sooner than I think. Finley smiled and turned to the menu. A few other guests had come into the restaurant—a man in his fifties with a pleasant Midwestern-esque face, and a couple, who until they spoke, looked very California. Finley marveled at how, even outside the US, she had a habit of attaching American attributes to people.

"What looks good to you?" Finley asked. The menu design—a picture of an *Alice in Wonderland* tea party with the Mad Hatter serving—was bizarre, but the dishes, predominantly biryanis and curries, smelled divine as they came from the kitchen.

"Want to share a vegetable curry?" Whitt said. "I know we're going to eat again tonight, but these look too good to pass up."

Having ordered, they settled into their corner seats and watched the world inside and outside. They could hear monkeys in the trees. They seemed to be waiting for morsels of food to be dropped close enough to the open doors that they could snatch up without the waiters seeing. The chatter inside the restaurant was almost as loud. Even though it was supposed to be the off-season, several minibuses of tour groups stopped at the hotel restaurant. Some to eat, others just to gawk at the Daliesque surroundings.

Whitt leaned in and whispered to Finley. "Who do you think is the killer?"

She was starting a round of the Murder Game, a story-building pastime that the two had played for years when they used to travel with their parents. The aim was to concoct intricate murder-mystery plots that involved the people they met during their travels, almost like a live version of Clue. Over the years, they had invented sordid affairs, failed romances, imminent financial ruin, and good old-fashioned greed as motives for murder by poisoning, bludgeoning, and gunshot. The sisters used to titter at breakfast over couples that they had maligned in their game the night before.

"Hard to say. What was the method and who was the victim?" Finley inquired.

"The man in the green shirt-khaki pants. Drowning—fell off a boat. Do you think his wife did it?" Whitt asked, keeping her face neutral and her voice modulated as she scanned the doorway through which the couple had entered.

A fragile-looking woman with an angelic face and feathery-blond curls stood beside the man looking at old photographs of the owner and her family that were plastered all over the wall. She looked more like a first-grade teacher than a woman who would push her husband off a speeding boat.

"No, I think it was his business partner." Finley replied just as their food arrived, spicing the air with coriander, fennel, cardamom, and cloves. All conversation ceased.

The ride into the hills from Helga's was a trip into another world. Even though it was only 75 kilometers away, the Montana, an architect's house that had been converted into a hideaway boutique hotel, was a little Shangri-La.

Finley and Whitt arrived just as the sun was painting the sky above the hills a soft blush-pink. The driveway into the hotel had been shadowed with green vines until it opened up to a pebbled walkway that ran along the side of an infinity pool. The pool reflected like a mirror a nearby banyan tree, the blush sky, and a golden dot in the heavens that was the retreating sun. Whitt and Finley stood on the manicured lawn and watched until the light of the sun was replaced by strategically placed fairy lights that gave the green a mythical aura.

"I expect Puck to run across the lawn any minute," Whitt joked.

"Yeah, do you think Lysander can mix a decent drink?"

"Let's freshen up and see."

The bellman showed the sisters to the largest of the four rooms in the hotel, setting their bags down and then pulling the blinds to reveal the beginnings of a curtain of stars, hung across the expansive night sky.

"Whenever you are ready, please let us serve you a welcome drink in the living room," the bellman said before he quietly closed the door.

By the time the sisters had freshened up and wandered into the common area, the other hotel guests had returned from their day of touring. A young, sunburned couple, perhaps on their honeymoon, fumbled up the stairs and waved hello as they headed to their room toward the back of the house. A few minutes later, they returned in cover-ups and bathing suits, carrying towels.

"A bit chilly for a dip, but it's a waste not to take advantage of the clear night," the gentleman said, as he asked the waiter to bring their drinks out to the pool. "Catch you later."

Finley nodded and kicked off her shoes. The cool of the stone-tiled floor sent a slight shiver through her. *I should be drinking a toddy to warm up. This wine is going to chill me straight through.* She got up and headed to the room to get a sweater.

"You want anything?" she asked as she passed Whitt. Whitt shook her head and went back to one of the glossy magazines on the ultramodern coffee table. As Finley entered the room, she saw the bamboo blind move. *Strange. No one here, but I could have sworn I closed that window. A monkey?* She double-checked the locks on the window, grabbed her sweater, and left again.

"I think we had visitors in our room," she said as she slid into the stylish, slate-colored leather seat. Whitt's eyes widened. "Probably monkeys, but we need to be sure that everything is locked up, so they don't walk off with my cameras or your jewelry!"

Dinner was like having a private chef at home. Whitt merely mentioned that she had a taste for fish, and the chef asked if she wanted to inspect the catch that was available for dinner that night. In the end, both sisters ended up settling on fish. Whitt asked for hers be grilled, and Finley opted for a fish curry in coconut milk. Around that time, the young couple joined them in the small dining area.

"How was your swim?" Whitt asked as they took their seats.

"Less of a swim and more of a wade," the young woman said in a broad Australian accent that sounded like extra syllables were being added to each word to an American ear. "The view of the stars was spectacular."

"Where are you from?" the young man inquired.

Finley and Whitt looked at each other. "It's complicated, but we are originally from the States," Whitt said. "Are you here on holiday?"

"Our honeymoon." Whitt and Finley had been right. This seemed the perfect place for a romantic getaway. "We climbed Sigiriya today. That was a haul. Are you going up?"

Finley nodded. Whitt had scheduled a couple of days in Kandy and other sites of the cultural triangle, using this hotel as a base. Sigiriya, with its twelve hundred steps, was on the list for tomorrow morning, with Polonnaruwa in the afternoon. A lot of driving, but it saved them having to change hotels. After a brief exchange of pleasantries about work and the weather, the couple turned their focus to placing their order, and Whitt and Finley concentrated on their dinner, which had just been served.

It wasn't until they were back in their room that the sisters began the Murder Game again. Whitt initiated it. "Do you think they had anything to do with that man's death?"

Finley had gotten dressed for bed and was propped up with pillows, reading a novel. She was initially caught off guard by the question. She stared at Whitt, her brow knitted. As she figured out the nature of Whitt's question, Finley's face relaxed.

"Can't say for sure. We need to figure out whether they have been together before—on a tour or in the same hotel. We need to establish opportunity."

"You always go by the book," Whitt smiled. "I just wing it. They're both young couples, so it's reasonable to assume that they would hang out at the lake together or on a water tour in Galle. There would be opportunity."

Finley yawned and put her book aside. "Well, I'm going to go by the book that says it's time for me to go to bed. And I'm *not* getting up before eight o'clock tomorrow," she said definitively as she clicked off the light.

Breakfast the next morning was a raucous affair because of a group of friendly monkeys that wanted to join Whitt, Finley, and the Campbells—the young Australian couple—for breakfast. As soon as the staff would shoo one monkey out, another two or three would run in to nab a muffin or piece of fruit from the sideboard. It looked like an episode featuring the Keystone Cops, and the monkeys had the upper hand.

Adesh, their driver, watched the scene play out from the veranda. He smiled at the monkeys' antics and soon put an end to it by luring one of the larger ones outside with a small banana. He threw pieces of the fruit over the terrace, and far down the hill once he had attracted the attention of the barrel. Some of the monkeys scurried after the banana, while the others waited to see what else might be offered.

To appease the rest, Adesh threw a small apple past the pool and into the jungle. Soon, there was only one small monkey left. It sat patiently waiting for its treat to be thrown. Instead, Adesh placed another small banana on the ledge near the large banyan so the little fellow could get the treat and head into the trees. With breakfast distributed, Adesh loaded a lunch basket and the sisters' backpacks into the car.

"Won't feeding them encourage that scavenging behavior?" Whitt asked.

Adesh tilted his head to make eye contact in his rear mirror and smiled. "Maybe, but not feeding them hasn't discouraged them, either."

As they drove along, the topography shifted from mountain to plains. Sigiriya, their first stop, rose from the flat plain like a massive, red stone table jutting up into the blue sky. The fifth-century rock fortress and King Kasyapa's royal residence were built on top of a Buddhist monastery. Sigiriya's 360-degree views used to once help the king ward off potential attackers. Now, it afforded everyone some of the most spectacular vistas of verdant jungle and distant mountains imaginable.

Tourists seemed to swarm the monument as the sisters ascended the narrow steel stairs that were attached precariously to the side of the rock face. Once they climbed the last step at the summit, however, Finley and Whitt felt small and alone against the enormity of the lush, green space that stretched out before them. It was no less breathtaking this time than it had been the last.

"If I had been the ruler of this kingdom, I would've been humbled by the expanse of humanity that lay before me," Whitt uttered as she took in the panoramic view. She and Finley were quiet, almost in reverence to the place.

As if the sky and earth were perfectly posed for a portrait, Finley was snapping away from the moment she and Whitt had gotten out of the car. She took shots of the massive lion's feet that sat at the base of the rock. She then held up the line of trekkers up the face in order to capture the ancient frescoes that graced the surface. But before she put her eye up to the viewfinder at the summit, she paused to drink in the majesty of the view. She was inclined to think that the ruins on the plateau used to be more like a monastery than a palace. There was indeed something sacred about the outcropping.

31

Once they were down the face of the rock, people sat to catch their breath on the benches that lined the walkway at the base of the rock. Finley and Whitt joined them, taking a seat on one of the shorter benches. The trees offered welcome shade from the sun that felt full force, even at that early hour in the day. Finley thought she saw several of the travelers that had stopped at Helga's the day before. *So much for this being better in the off-season. I hope the highlands are less crowded.*

By the time they reached Polonnaruwa some three hours later, Whitt and Finley felt reenergized by the sumptuous lunch provided by the Montana. There had been grilled chicken seasoned to perfection with cumin and coriander, pickled vegetables and parathas, and fresh fruit rolled in chili for dessert. They had sat among a small cluster of rocks and trees just off the road and watched the day-to-day life of the village go by—young girls with long pigtails tied at the ends with ribbons and their sari-draped mothers walking along the road, bodies swaying in rhythm; men on bicycles weighed down with weekly supplies; and brightly painted trucks loaded with sacks of foodstuffs.

Polonnaruwa, the ruins of an ancient civilization from thousands of years ago, was everything Finley had remembered from the trip to the area some three years before. In places, the UNESCO World Heritage site was little more than crumbling, reddish stones strewn across a path. Elsewhere, the stones were stacked into pillars that suggested entryways to majestic buildings. It was when she stepped back from the individual collection of stones and surveyed the area that she saw the blueprint of a city that would have rivaled Rome in size and architectural beauty.

The afternoon sun was playing tricks with shadows on the green of the overgrowth and the black-brown crust on the rotting pillars. Carved-stone thresholds in half-moon arches announced residential areas, while statues of elephants, dragons, and monkeys signaled official buildings. The dancing shadows from the nearby tree leaves gave life to a city that had long been dead. Whitt sat on an ancient stone bench and watched as Finley, fascinated by the light on the stones, captured shot after shot, composing some magic canvas in her head.

"I know that I don't have your photographer's eye, but what are you seeing that I'm not? It just looks like lines and lines of old stones. Beautiful, and while I appreciate the history of it, don't they all start to look the same after a while?" Whitt was staring perplexedly at her sister, who had dropped to one knee to get a better angle of the light through the stone pillars.

Finley chuckled to herself. *That's what Great-Aunt Sally had said about the castles in Germany. Once you've seen one, you've seen them all.*

"I'm just hoping that one of these many shots will reveal something compelling. Something that I didn't see when I clicked the shutter," she replied. *Serendipity. Like the shot of the elephant spray.*

"Let's go," Finley lowered the camera. "I can tell you are getting bored. And I'm getting stiff."

Their timing couldn't have been better. Two minivans loaded with German tourists pulled up just as Finley and Whitt headed back toward the car. It was clear from the looks on their faces that they were more in Whitt's school of thought than Finley's. To them, Polonnaruwa was a pile of rubble. Finley had stopped near the car to use her telephoto lens on a grouping of pillars. By the time she finished, the vans had loaded back up and were pulling off.

"I pity their driver," Whitt said. "I'm not that bad, am I?"

Finley smiled. "Nah, you at least count to one hundred before you're ready to go. So, thanks for indulging me. I don't know why I love this place so much."

"Neither do I," Whitt mumbled under her breath as she climbed into the car.

Finley slept for the better part of the trip back to the hotel. When she woke up, she found that Whitt had joined her nap. The climb up Sigiriya, the heavy lunch, and the walk around Polonnaruwa had sapped their energy. A dip in the pool and a quiet dinner seemed in order.

Back at the hotel, the sisters nodded to the staff as they made their way to their room. Whitt had just opened the door when she looked up and stepped back. "What the…" she said.

Finley was close behind so she could see what had given Whitt pause. The room had been ransacked, but only a portion of it. The beds and night table were just as pristine as when they had left. The closet had also been left closed. However, the books, magazines, and papers that had been on the desk were scattered about, ripped, and shredded. *Monkeys. Again.*

"I know I left that window locked. You saw me check it," Finley said. "After last night, I was careful."

"Those little buggers are sneaky," Whitt said. "I'll get the housekeeper to come clean it. Check to see if anything is missing."

The houseboy, a young man of about sixteen or so, apologized repeatedly for the mess the monkeys had made. He checked the window and saw that it was indeed locked shut. He was puzzled, his face darting between the locked window and the destruction in the room. Finally, he just shook his head and started picking up the shreds of paper thrown about.

The sisters had concluded that besides the itinerary, which could easily be reprinted, there was nothing of real value lost in the debris. They grabbed their backpacks and headed to the living room for drinks while their room was cleaned.

"We should still be able to get to the pool before the sun sets," Finley said. The sun was just about eye level in the sky. She took a few random shots of the flowers, the stupas on the far hills, and the monkeys. Whitt had already kicked off her shoes and dipped her feet into the cool water, her drink by her side.

The waiter brought their second round to the pool. Once the room was clean, the sisters slipped into their swimsuits and grabbed their towels. They were the only ones in the hotel tonight as the Campbells had left earlier in the day, so they dispensed with cover-ups. The water was surprisingly warm, still heated by the sun. They waded to the edge of the pool, faced the sunset, and watched as the heavens were once again painted pink and the sun seemed to withdraw into the evening sky.

"That was nice," Whitt said.

"This is nice," Finley added, raising her glass. "Thanks for a special birthday. I don't think it can get much better than this."

4

THE TRAIN FROM KANDY TO Nuwara Eliya snaked through stunning highland countryside. Whitt and Finley had decided on the early train that left just before nine o'clock in the morning. The air was still cool, and mist hung between the trees as the train wove around the hills and across the deep ravines that dimpled the landscape. Both sides of the train were treated to breathtaking scenery. Finley moved back and forth between her seat in the first-class cabin and the corridor outside that ran the length of the car, trying to catch the twenty shades of green, the depth of the terraced hills, and the alternating rough and smooth textures of the tableau laid out in front of her.

Whitt read from the guidebook as her sister sidled past her to lean her lens on the opened window frame. "The train runs on the original 1864 rails laid by the British during their time overseeing the island. The train passes through tunnel after tunnel, opening onto spectacular waterfalls and lush green tea plantations," Whitt read, periodically glancing out at the passing landscape. *Hope they serviced these tracks recently. That's a long way down.*

"Do they mention how friendly the Sri Lankan people are?" Finley asked. "It's like a personal welcoming committee, all the smiling and waving."

The train had slowed just enough that as they entered a tunnel, Finley was able to grab a shot of a shy little girl sticking her head out from around a tree to wave at the passing train. Her smile was all the lighting the shot needed. *That's going to be one I keep for a while. I wish Mama could have seen her. She would have melted—after she did something with the child's hair. Mama and well-brushed hair.*

Adesh met them at the station outside Nuwara Eliya. From the looks of it—namely the several cups stacked around him that had most likely once been filled with milk tea—he had been there for a while. He had driven the car with their luggage the 76 kilometers from Kandy to Nuwara Eliya while the train ambled along close to 200 kilometers of track. An hour plus for Adesh compared to their four hours. But the trip by train had been worth it.

"Did you enjoy?" Adesh asked, smiling as they alighted from the train.

Whitt nodded toward Finley. "She was in heaven, hanging out of the door even to get shots. She was grinning from ear to ear."

The short ride to the hotel took them through Nuwara Eliya itself, a small scenic town that was an oasis away from the heat of Colombo for the British who lived on the island.

The Sandford House, their hotel for the next several days, was a tea planter's residence that had been renovated and converted into a small guesthouse. One traveled from the graveled driveway through an arched picket fence, around planter boxes with petunias and geraniums to a grassy green that looked out onto terraces of tea plants. The inside of the house reminded Whitt of a hunting lodge with its vaulted, wood ceiling beams and stone fireplace. The sweet smell of fresh pastries caught Finley's attention. She hadn't realized until then that she was getting a bit peckish, as the Brits say.

"Welcome, welcome!" came a cheery voice with a British accent from a room just beyond the front entry. A middle-aged woman, whose countenance matched her voice, greeted them with a dish towel in one hand and plate of freshly baked hand pies in the other. "I'm Harriet. You're just in time for tea. Unless you would prefer coffee."

She laughed as if her statement was the joke of the year. She put the pastries on a table positioned in front of a bay window that took up almost the entire living room wall. The window looked out onto a rose garden where bushes hung heavy with colorful blossoms in full bloom. Beyond that were layers upon layers of tiered tea plants.

"You're right in the middle of a working tea planation," she said. "So, you will see tea pickers in the fields at various times of the day, and then the throngs of hikers and tourists on the trails that run just outside the hedges. There's fencing inside the hedges, so don't worry about security."

"I'm assuming you are the Blake sisters," she continued. "We have a pretty healthy contingent of guests for the next few days. It will be nice."

Finley muttered to herself. *Nice for whom? I hope they are out wandering all day so I can chill out.* Harriet was now showing them their room, which was spacious, but with the kind of comfortable decor that suggested guests spend more time in the common areas than in the rooms.

"When you get washed up, come out and have your tea," Harriet said. "The others should be coming in from their wanderings shortly."

Whitt and Finley were sitting on the green at a teak table laden with pastries and their tea when the other guests started filtering in. Whitt had moved the umbrella over so that they could use the heat of the sun to warm themselves in the cool mountain air. The hand pies, stuffed with cinnamon-spiced pineapple bits, were heavenly, and the tea was strong and rich.

"My, that looks good." A slender young British woman in her early thirties was standing near their table. She had been so silent in her approach that they hadn't noticed her until that moment. *Colette, that Armstrong girl who lived near grandma, used to do that.*

Sneak up on you without making a sound, catlike. Unsettling, Finley remembered.

"Hello. Did you have a good walk?" Finley found her voice first. The woman was pleasant looking, but not strikingly beautiful or anything. She was what Americans would peg as typically British: rather thin, twig-brown hair with bewitching blue eyes. She wore sneakers, khakis, and a sweater, but she had pushed up the sleeves as if it had gotten too warm. On one wrist, Finley noticed a medical bracelet. *Wonder what that's for? Diabetes? Allergies? MS?*

"Yes, I think I walked the length of the property," she laughed lightly. "I may actually have ventured onto the next plantation. It's just so peaceful here." She wandered off into the house, leaving the thought unfinished.

Whitt raised an eyebrow and looked at Finley. "A bit airheaded, that one."

Finley had just taken a bite of a hand pie when the next guest returned. He was more obvious in his approach and more American in his manner.

"Hello! Harriet said there would be more Americans coming. I never would have picked you out as American though, the way you're dressed. French maybe." He talked on for a while before he paused to introduce himself.

"Aren't I being rude!" The man stuck his hand out to Whitt. "Tom Allendale."

"Whitt Blake. And this is my sister, Finley," Whitt offered. She had sized the man up as being a middle-aged insurance agent from Des Moines whose wife had divorced him, and he had decided to take the trip that was supposed to be for their twenty-fifth wedding anniversary anyway.

He turned and offered his hand to Finley. His handshake was firm, but not aggressive. He had sandy-brown hair with a bit of gray that was combed into a fifth-grade side part. His soft brown eyes smiled genuinely, reflecting a natural friendliness. He was attractive in a settled sort of way. Finley could imagine that he had been considered good-looking at one time, but either a tragedy or time added a layer of sadness that smothered the brightness necessary to make him conventionally handsome.

"I'm going to run in and get cleaned up so I can get some of that." He nodded at the small plate of half-eaten hand pies and headed into the house.

"We are going to have such fun at our Game with this crew," Whitt whispered as she smiled slyly. She had always been better at the Game than Finley, thinking up ghoulish murders that were cleverly executed. *Hope this girl always stays on the right side of the law. If not, they are going to have a hard time catching her. She might actually get away with it*, Finley thought.

Finley returned the smile with a slight shake of her head. Groups of walkers were trickling in past the hedges, presumably coming back from treks and heading in for tea at their respective hotels and guesthouses. From what she could tell, there was little else to do up in tea country besides tour, taste, and walk.

That was fine with both Whitt and Finley. Finley needed to think through the details of her plan for India and she needed to ferret out what was up with Whitt and David. Whitt still hadn't mentioned anything—but since she had been in Sri Lanka, she also hadn't connected on FaceTime or WhatsApp as far as Finley knew.

Finley saw some faces among the walkers that she recognized from the train and other sites in Colombo and Kandy. She looked over at Whitt and saw her staring into the distance. *I bet she is playing the Game. Her face is too focused for her to be daydreaming. I wonder who she's written in.*

"Who's involved this time?" Finley asked, her eyes still fixed on the lush green slopes just over the hedge. Most of the pickers had headed back to have their bags weighed, but a few lingered, presumably hoping to add a few more pounds of weight so that they could get a higher price for their work. As Harriet had explained, the pickers were paid by weight, so just a few more pounds in their bags could mean significantly more rupees.

"How'd you know?"

"I've lived with you in my orbit for almost thirty years. I know."

"I've seen some of these people before, so I figured I'd make them part of the Game." Whitt was surveying a cluster of couples ambling by. "That gentleman there with the walking stick. He reminds me of a Prussian prince. I'm assuming the woman is his wife. They've actually assumed the identities of a wealthy Austrian couple who died in an avalanche last winter."

"How'd they do that?" Finley's face was twisted into an incredulous frown. "Most importantly, why would they do that?"

"They were both in the same chalet, and they switched papers with them," Whitt was quietly sipping her tea. Finley had turned to face her, the puzzled look still on her face. *Sometimes you just don't know people. Where does she come up with these things?*

"That easy, eh? But you still haven't said why."

"Because they could! Why be poor when you can be rich?" Whitt was looking at Finley intently. "They had the chance of slipping into a rich person's identity and living well."

"And then what? They're surely going to get caught."

"At a certain point, they kill themselves off again. After they've stashed some money," Whitt said. "And then they go off to an uninhabited island and live out the rest of their lives."

Finley had leaned forward, staring at her sister, her mouth slightly open, amazed at her sister's imagination. "Have you ever considered this?"

"No! Why would I?" Whitt seemed disgusted by the thought. "What I create in my mind and what I would actually consider are two very different things!"

Finley sat back, "So then how do they relate to the poor guy who got pushed off the boat?"

"We'll just have to figure that out now, won't we?" Whitt had gotten to her feet and picked up the teapot. "More of the same?" Finley nodded.

Harriet and the chef—they had assumed there was someone in the kitchen in addition to Harriet—outdid themselves at dinner. There were only two entrées each night to choose from, but the preparation rivaled that at the Montana. The selections that night were devilled chicken and fish in banana leaf. The sisters decided to have one of each so that they could taste both of the new dishes.

They were the first ones in the dining room, deciding to enjoy a glass of wine at the table rather than in one of the sitting rooms. Harriet had brought them glasses of champagne and put a nice off-dry Riesling in a bucket of ice to chill. Finley was surprised that the guesthouse had a decent selection of wines. She originally assumed she would end up drinking Lion beer for most of the time in Nuwara Eliya.

Finley and Whitt were glad they had asked where to sit before stationing themselves at a table since it appeared that the other guests had their "regular" tables. The young British woman had been the next guest in. Without speaking, she had moved to a table for two along the back wall. She was casually dressed but looked stylish in a skirt and sweater tunic—a contrast to the walking togs she had worn when they first met. Tom, the American, came in next and took a similar table on the side wall nearest the door. Both nodded to each other and to the sisters before placing their orders and picking up their books. *I like this crew. They know how to give people space.* Finley observed.

Harriet had just come to take away their champagne flutes and open the bottle of white when the final guests came in. They were a middle-aged couple that could have been from the UK or any of the former colonies—the US, Scotland, Ireland, Australia, or South Africa. The woman, a grandmotherly type in her mid-sixties with a frizzy cap of gray-streaked, light-brown curls, went first to Tom to say her hellos before heading over to the young woman. She then turned her attention to Finley and Whitt.

"Well, hello and welcome!" Whitt couldn't place her accent other than to say she was British. "Hope you are settling in. Have you met Samantha and Tom?" She turned to indicate the two other diners.

"I'm Helen and that's my husband, Richard," she continued. "We're the Lockes from Loch Ness." She paused to laugh at her own joke. "No, really, we're from Bibury in the Cotswolds." Her husband had taken a seat at a table not far from where she was standing.

Finley nodded to her husband, who smiled in return. He seemed used to his wife's outgoing nature and occupied himself with looking over the offerings of the day. Harriet came out with two tall glasses of beer without even needing to take the Lockes' order.

"I'd better go before my beer goes flat." She headed over to the table and sat. She exchanged a few words with her husband before turning back to Finley and Whitt.

"What are your names, by the way? And where're you from?"

"I'm Finley and this is my sister, Whitt. We're from the States."

"How long are you going to be here?"

"At the guest house or in Sri Lanka?" Whitt asked, taking a sip of her wine and looking over at the couple. She was trying to place them. She thought she had seen the husband in one of the several tour groups they had run into over the past few days. His shock of reddish-brown hair stood out.

"Here at the lodge."

"A few days and then we head to Galle."

"Is this your first time in Sri Lanka?"

"No, we were here a couple of years ago but didn't get to see everything we wanted to," Finley fielded the final question. Their dinner had arrived during the conversation, and the sisters had been waiting for a lull before they tucked into their food.

"Leave them to eat their supper, Helen!" It was the first time Whitt or Finley had heard Richard's voice. It was a rich, deep baritone, like that of an opera singer. Finley thought briefly of Evans, the Interpol inspector who had helped them in Morocco, who also had a melodious voice.

The wife apologized, nodding her permission for them to start eating. She and her husband instead carried on a rather one-sided conversation, with her asking questions that she answered herself before he could respond. Whitt arched an eyebrow and smiled as she took a bite of the elegantly seasoned fish. *Poor man can't get a word in. If we find her smothered in her sleep, I won't say a thing. The guy deserves some peace.*

5

T HE NEXT MORNING, WHITT AND Finley found themselves glad they had taken their walk around the tea fields early in the morning because by noon, light misty rain fell on the hills. Only the heartiest of hikers were seen on the trails when rainfall started in earnest. The pickers who had gone out as early as four in the morning had come in when the rains got heavier. The December to late-March period was generally dry and cool—the best time to harvest leaves in the highlands, so the rain was unusual.

"I hope it doesn't rain too long." Harriet was at the window looking out to the lush terraces whose green had deepened with the moisture. "The pickers need at least a few more weeks."

Finley, Whitt, and most of the other guests had gathered in the living room with books or iPads to take advantage of the lazy day to decompress from the previous days of touring. Harriet had had one of the staff members make a fire in the fireplace, which took off some of the chill. Tom had retired to one of the smaller sitting rooms to do some work. It turned out that he wasn't an insurance agent from Des Moines, but rather a lawyer from Pittsburgh who needed to finish reviewing a contract so he could get back to enjoying his vacation. Whitt and Finley had established themselves on one of the sofas near the fireplace. The Lockes had moved away from the fire, saying it was a bit too warm for them. Samantha had joined them on the other side of the room, preferring the coolness of the far corner.

"I like nippy days like today. Reminds me of home," Helen said. "In some parts of the country, you have to keep a small fire going for most of the year."

Samantha nodded and smiled, mentioning how much the high country of Sri Lanka reminded her of parts of England. Indeed, Nuwara Eliya and the nearby area were sometimes called Little England because of the cool misty climate and the turn-of-the-century houses that had been built to look like a fairy-tale English village. Whitt and Samantha continued the conversation for a while after Whitt commented on the chic, suede walking boots Samantha had on.

Eventually, Whitt and Finley pulled out their books and tossed aside their shoes, lounging their tall, lean bodies in front of the fire. While her eyes were on her book, Finley knew Whitt's mind was elsewhere. *Is she still playing that Game or is she thinking of something—no, someone—else?*

"What're you thinking about?" Finley decided a direct approach was probably best with Whitt. "Is that book that thought provoking? You look like you're pondering the challenges of the universe."

Whitt looked away from the fire and smiled, "Was I drifting again? I can't even remember. I guess I just need to clear my mind."

She turned her body on the sofa to look out the window. The rain had stopped, and the sun was trying hard to peek through. A few more tourists were wandering along the trails.

"Want to go for a walk?" Whitt asked. "I think I need some fresh air."

Finley nodded and slipped her shoes back on. "Let me grab a jacket and my camera. You want anything from the room?"

"Nope. I have my shawl. I think that and my sweater should be enough." She got up and wrapped herself in a richly embroidered Kashmiri pashmina shawl in grays and teals. She drew closer to the fire as Finley headed to the room.

When Finley returned, Whitt was already outside on the green with her face turned to catch the sun. Finley waved to the others and headed out to join her.

"Which way do you want to go?" Finley asked.

"Let's take the upper trails."

The upper trails wrapped around the back of the hill that was most visible from the Sandford and along a crest that ran up to a lookout point at the edge of the property. Harriet had said that that was an overseer's watch that had a bird's eye view of most of the plantation and the adjoining properties.

Their walk along the trail was evenly paced, with Finley taking time at various points to catch shots of the tea terraces. While light and angle had been her focus in Morocco, here she played with light and color. If Morocco had been about edges, Sri Lanka was about curves, and with the curves came the nuances of color on the hills, along the trails, and even in the undulations of the leaves.

About one hour into the walk, they had almost reached the overseer's watch and neither had yet uttered a single word. Finley had been absorbed in her work, so she let Whitt keep her silence. Frankly, she didn't know what to say because she didn't know what, if anything, was wrong. She would have to wait this one out and hope that Whitt would open the door to a conversation. The waiting worked.

"What do you want to know?" Whitt said softly—so softly that Finley almost didn't hear her.

"Whatever you want to share."

"Nothing is really wrong, and yet everything is," Whitt started to cry. A single silent tear had slipped out, starting a dam burst that prompted them to sit down in the overseer's watch.

Again, Finley waited. She wanted to comfort her sister, but she knew that Whitt's independence meant she would shrug off a sympathetic arm or reassuring hand. So, Finley sat on the hard bench and waited, her eyes fixed on her sister's dropped head.

"He wants to get married," Whitt finally muttered, the words muffled by the long hair that blocked her face.

Finley's eyes widened, and her brow furrowed. She was trying to figure out the "wrong" part of this picture. David and Whitt seemed so well suited for each other. The guy handled her sister's moods with loving deftness, parried her barbed tongue with a sharp wit, and pierced through her armor to reveal her soft side like no one else had ever done.

"Help me understand," was all Finley could manage to say.

"He's almost thirty and he wants to settle down and have a family."

"And you don't?"

"I do, but…" Whitt's voiced tailed off.

"But?"

"But I don't know if I'm ready to settle down now. I want to keep traveling, living overseas, trying new things."

"And he doesn't?"

"I don't know. When I heard the word 'marry,' my brain stopped," Whitt muttered.

"So, you don't know what his notion of married life looks like? Don't you think it's pretty important for you two to define that before you get coltish and run off?"

Finley thought back on her own first marriage. She and Grant Lambert, a fellow lawyer, had assumed that they both had the same vision of married life. But it turned out that they hadn't. He had wanted a house in Greenwich with a picket fence and stairstep kids. She had wanted a life as an expat, living in far-off places. They had to divorce to get what they both needed.

"I'm afraid to have that conversation. What if our ideas are so different that it won't work out?" Whitt had looked up, her eyes begging Finley for an answer that would soothe her soul.

"Well, you won't know until you ask, and all this speculating is killing you. Probably killing him too," Finley said. "You've seen what 'failure to communicate' does to relationships. And people. Let Max and me be a lesson to you."

Finley and Max had spent three years apart, loving each other but believing that the other didn't care and not knowing why. Only a series of recent encounters in Tangier had forced them to talk openly enough to realize the loss they had both experienced because of their assumptions.

"You've got to play the hand all the way out. No matter how much it hurts," Finley said.

"You don't fold because you think you'll lose. You play because you think you might win," Whitt continued. "I'm folding, eh?"

Finley nodded, a wistful smile on her lips, "You have to play, kid."

She stood and pulled her camera back out of her bag. *She just needs to think this all through. She'll come up with a plan of action in her typically efficient way. They'll figure it out. Max and I have. For now.*

Finley smiled to herself and started taking shots of the cascading tiers of green. Some of the pickers had come back out, pulling rain tarps off the tender green plants, their brightly colored clothing contrasted against the sea of green.

She took a series of shots with one set of lenses, and then started playing with different filters as the clouds finally broke and the sun started to shine brightly. The filters allowed her to capture more of the variations of green that painted the hills—a forest green beside a Kelly green, against a hunter green and a shade of fern green. She also used her telephoto lens to catch snatches of walkers among the tea terraces. She thought she saw the Lockes and Samantha, as well as some other couples that had passed them on the trails near the guesthouse. Some, she assumed, were with the German tour groups that kept popping up. Traveling with a tour group would be a kiss of death to her.

"What can you see from here besides an ocean of green?" Whitt had gotten up and was standing near her sister. *I hope she has decided*

49

to have the "talk." Finley reached into her pack and passed Whitt a pair of binoculars without taking her face out from behind the camera. "A galaxy of green. If green isn't your color, you'd have a hard time around here," Finley laughed. "I'm getting hungry. Is it teatime?"

Whitt checked her watch. "By the time we walk down—seeing that you'll want to photograph all the caterpillars and rain trickles—we might just be able to catch the end of it!" *Her humor is back. That's a good sign.*

On the way back, they decided to take a different trail, one that ran near the picker village. Finley had wanted to grab candid shots of the pickers, their families, and the conditions in which they lived. Many had taken over old British soldier barracks, painted them bright colors and decorated them with local symbols. However lovely they looked from the outside, they couldn't paper over the outside toilets and open sewers that ran near where children played with soccer balls made from trash bags. Finley's shutter clicked nonstop as she and Whitt walked by. "Harriet said that there is a clinic and a school at this location, which is rare for picker villages," Finley said.

"Better. But they still live in poverty," Whitt cast a sad sideglance at the village and trudged back toward the Sandford. Finley followed, after catching a few parting shots. *She and Max are a lot alike. Cursing the wind even as they tilt at windmills. I guess a lifetime doing development work can do that to you.*

It took them a few minutes upon getting back to reconcile the pungent smells of the picker village lingering in their nostrils with the homey sweetness of teatime that was already underway. The sisters washed up quickly and headed back out to the green with their tea and sandwiches to take advantage of the sunshine. Tom had taken a break from his work and claimed a seat near the rose garden.

"Please come join me," he said, pulling out chairs for both women. "Did you have a nice walk? How far did you go?"

Whitt described the trek up to the overseer watch and the walk past the picker village.

"I've stuck to the lower trails thus far. Haven't gone up," he said. "I will have to do that tomorrow, if it doesn't rain. Have you done the tea factory tour yet?"

"Not yet. Have you?" Finley asked. "Which ones are the best?"

Tom described his experience at the tea factories that he had visited and suggested two that were especially good—one for tasting and another for their thorough explanation of the process.

"You can ask Harriet to book it for you, and you can do both in a day." Tom went on to describe the tea-making process and the different types of tea made. He had done tea tasting in China and India but considered the tea in Sri Lanka to be some of the best.

"Need to get back to work," he lamented. "I only have one more day of vacation. I want to get this contract finished so I can enjoy my last few hours of R&R."

Samantha wasn't at dinner, and neither was Tom, but the Lockes were seated and already mid-course when Finley and Whitt entered the dining room. The selections were cottage pie or baked fish. Again, the sisters chose one of each and ordered a bottle of wine.

"How did your day go, ladies?" Helen asked. "Did you go far on your walk?"

"Just to the overseer's watch and back," Finley said. "What did you do?"

"We just stuck around here the whole day," Helen said. "It was too wet for me, and Richard took a nap."

Whitt and Finley exchanged glances. Finley was about to probe further but thought better of it. Something wasn't right, but she didn't know the Lockes well enough to challenge their version of events. She was sure she had seen them this afternoon on the trails, but she could be wrong.

"What are you up to tomorrow?" Richard asked.

"We think we'll go on a couple of factory tours. Tom mentioned several that were good, and we asked Harriet to book us."

"We haven't decided what we are doing, but we may do a tour or two, too. We've met some folks whose tour schedule in Sri Lanka matches ours, so we have been coordinating with them. Who knows?" Helen said.

She and Richard rose and collected their room key and eyeglasses from the table. The room key was attached to a compact key ring that looked like it had both a small flashlight and a thumb drive on it. *I need to ask them where they got that. It is cute and practical.* The Lockes nodded as they headed out towards the living room.

"That's a bit odd. Why did they lie about where they were?" Whitt had reached over to try some of Finley's fish and stopped her fork mid-arc to put the question to her sister.

"I know. You saw them and so did I. You can't miss his hair."

"Do you think we'll get that addled when we are older?"

"I don't think it's addled as much as obfuscating." Finley sat quietly looking into her wine glass. She was mentally lining up facts to see if there were other things that didn't add up.

"Whatever it is, we're not getting involved," Whitt said. "There is no Evans to bail us out this time."

Adesh met them just after breakfast for the short trip to Newton Tea Factory, one of the smaller tea plantations and processing facility in Nuwara Eliya. Tom and Harriet had both pegged this tour as better for the tasting than the tour, though the tour itself proved informative. The tour guide had taken them out to the terraced field so that they could see how the tea was picked. Two leaves and a bud. That was all that was taken from each plant. If pickers went further down the plant, the leaves were tougher, and the tea quality was compromised.

After the brief tour of the field and the factory floor, the sisters were invited to the tasting room. There were only two others on the tour, a British couple from London, who were staying at the

Heritance Tea Factory, an old tea-processing factory that had been converted into a hotel.

The guide had made tea from lower-altitude plantations near Kandy and compared the color and taste with those from Nuwara Eliya so that they could see the difference that altitude makes. The dark-reddish hue of the low-grown teas contrasted sharply with the straw-colored brew from the high-grown leaves. She also allowed the tasters to compare the delicate flavor of white tea with the rich taste of black teas as she explained the differences in picking and preparation.

When they left, Whitt and Finley had several packages of teas in their satchels, some for their drinking pleasure and some to take home as gifts. The packaging alone, brocade sacs with vibrant cording, was gift worthy.

They had a couple of hours before the next tea factory tour started, so they had Adesh drive them into downtown Nuwara Eliya. Adesh dropped them in front of the post office, a beautiful Tudor building that reflected the architecture found around most of the town. From there, they wandered through the picturesque streets of chalet-like buildings until they reached the Grand Hotel, a *grande dame* of luxury hotels built in the old European style early in the last century.

While they sipped champagne and snacked on samosas, Finley scrolled through the shots she had taken over the past few days. She was starting to feel more confident in her ability to capture on film what was in her mind's eye. She was also more willing to experiment with the lenses and filters that were becoming part of her regular tool kit. While she looked through the frames, she kept an eye out for pictures of the Lockes.

"There. That's definitely Richard and the woman with him looks just like Helen. The time stamp says it was yesterday." Finley held the camera over so Whitt could see.

"Just keep those frames safe in case something happens involving them and the police are brought in," Whitt said. "But besides that, keep your mouth shut. We don't have any backup. No Max. No David. No Evans. Not even Taylor, assuming that there is something amiss. Maybe we just read too many mysteries!"

Finley laughed and nodded. They had gotten sucked into a few dicey situations in Morocco but had had backup, as Whitt said. She thought of the people that had had their backs then—Max and David, of course. But there had also been Evans, the seasoned inspector from Interpol and his assistant, Taylor. She smiled when she thought of Taylor. He was young and sometimes bumbling, but he had proven a sure shot when it mattered. In Sri Lanka, they knew no one.

A short but scenic drive from town brought the sisters to the next tea planation. The tour of the Nine Arch Tea Factory, one of the oldest and largest on the island, started with another trip to the fields. This time, however, the guide sent the twenty or so tourists into the field with a picker, who showed them how to pick before letting each person get a feel for the technique by picking themselves. Finley and Whitt each got a chance to pinch their two leaves and a bud, finding it more difficult than it appeared. Finley had an easier time getting some candid shots of Whitt, deep in concentration as she picked.

Whitt and Finley followed the group onto the factory floor. Whitt saw the Lockes and two of the couples from the German group that stopped at Polonnaruwa. She also saw the Campbells and nodded in their direction when she made eye contact. They smiled in return. The guide was explaining the different types of machines that ran in the factory.

"The drying machine here is one of our older machines. It is smaller, too." She pointed to the large, two-story processing machines that took up the rear two-thirds of the massive factory building. "But this one is open-sided so you can easily see the tea moving on the belts through the dryer."

She was midway through her explanation of the withering and drying process when two workers came running from the mountain of machines in the back, screaming and talking rapidly in Sinhala. The guide stopped and went to the small office off the entry way. Finley and Whitt assumed that that was the plant manager's office, and that someone must be hurt.

"Please stay here. Do not move from this area," the guide said when she returned. "There has been an accident, and we must take care of it."

She repeated herself, a bit more sternly this time. "Please do not move from this area."

The group began to mutter among themselves, speculating on the nature of the accident.

"Do you think one of the workers has fallen into one of the machines?" someone asked.

"They must have safeguards against that," another responded. The theories grew more outrageous as the time went on.

It took a few minutes, but soon the sound of sirens could be heard in the distance. As the sirens grew louder, the guide moved the group over to the side so that the paramedics could get through. All she would say in response to questions about what happened was that there had been an accident.

The ambulance team, two paramedics and a driver, pushed a gurney through the front door and headed toward the back of the factory floor. Many of the workers that were in other parts of the building now crowded around the front entrance, craning their necks for a view. The guide still refused to say more than that the group needed to stay put until the ambulance left.

Shortly, more sirens were heard in the distance. The tour group pushed forward to see if another ambulance was arriving. Instead, it was three police cars, all with sirens blaring. Two police officers got out of the first car, came through the door, and were directed to the back of the factory. Within minutes, three more officers arrived. One of those officers moved more deliberately, surveying the crowd as he walked toward the apparent scene of the accident.

"He's probably the inspector," Whitt whispered to Finley, who nodded in agreement. "What do you think is going on? You don't call the cops for an accident."

"Unless it's a foreigner, and you're covering your tail," Finley said. Finley was glad for her height. She could see over many in the group and if she angled herself, she could see down the factory floor to where a group of people was gathered. They appeared to be looking into a machine, or at least into the underbelly of a machine. *God, I hope no one fell in. That would be a bloody mess.*

The inspector-looking officer was now on his knees looking into the machine. One of the officers was taking pictures and, on command, another one of the officers reached into the machine and pulled out what looked to be a body. It wasn't moving. The paramedics moved in and appeared to check for a pulse. There was a shake of the head, and the ambulance team began to put the body on the gurney and cover it with a sheet.

Finley was struck by the lack of blood. There appeared to be no blood on the body, on the officer who pulled the body out, or on the paramedics who handled the body. If it had been an industrial accident, there should have been blood.

"When they wheel the gurney out, look for blood anywhere on the covering," Finley whispered to Whitt.

She went back up on tiptoe to get a better view. They were starting to move the body down the corridor to the front entry way. The police had cordoned off the area with yellow tape. *Whitt is going to ask her question about the universality of yellow police tape again. Unless she already found the answer.*

As the body came parallel with her, Finley gasped. Several in the group turned to look at her, including Whitt.

"What is it?" Whitt asked, seeing Finley go pale.

The inspector had also heard Finley's reaction and approached her. The crowd parted and the man stood before her, looking at her curiously. "Do you know this person or something about what happened?"

He was about her height and reed thin with piercing dark eyes and a thin mustache that looked like it had been penciled on. His gaze never wavered from hers as he waited for her response.

"I don't know. I can't see her face, but I think I recognized the bracelet. One of the guests at the guesthouse we're staying in wore a medical bracelet like that. Those bracelets are common, but…" Finley's voice trailed off.

"Can you come with me?" The man took her by the elbow and guided her toward the entrance.

"Not without me, she can't!" Whitt was right on Finley's heels. She grabbed her other arm.

"And who are you, madam?"

"Her sister. She's not going anywhere without me unless you want an international incident." Whitt was getting red in the face.

"She is not a suspect, as far as I know. So, I have no problem with you accompanying her," the man said. "I just need her statement."

"Then we will follow you in our car." Finley had regained her voice. The inspector started to hesitate and then relented. "Can you tell me where we are going, so I can inform my driver?"

The inspector accompanied the sisters over to the car where Adesh sat waiting. He spoke to him in Sinhala and Adesh nodded.

"Then I will see you at the station. I am Inspector Dev Perera. And your names?" Finely and Whitt gave the inspector their names and where they were staying.

"And the name of the young woman you suspect this to be?"

"Samantha. I don't know her last name," Finley said softly. Whitt turned and stared at Finley in disbelief. Samantha was dead.

6

THE NUWARA POLICE STATION WAS a nondescript stucco cube tucked behind the beautiful Tudor chalets that lined the main street. Men in dark khaki uniforms with various degrees of gold braid on their shoulders moved in and out of dark, window-less rooms that held multiple arrangements of gray metal tables and chairs. To Whitt and Finley's surprise, they were shown into one of few offices with windows and a proper wooden desk.

"Please have a seat. Can we offer you a tea or water?" The inspector paused, "We may have coffee somewhere around here. I would have to check."

"Some wa—" Finley started to ask for water and then thought better of it. If they had to stay for any period of time at the station, using a communal toilet with an iffy stomach would not be pleasant. "On second thought, tea, please." Whitt requested the same.

The inspector went to the door and asked one of the men roaming up and down the halls for three cups of tea. He then called down the hall in an abrupt tone. Shortly, a fresh-faced young man with no braid scurried into the room, shut the door, and took his seat beside the inspector. He opened a small spiral pad of paper and looked up.

"So, may we have your names again and where are you staying? So my friend here can capture it?" The inspector had put his glasses halfway up his nose and was peering over the top of them.

Whitt and Finley gave their names and the street address of the Sandford. "I don't know the number," Whitt said.

"No matter. We know where it is," the inspector said. "You say this lady that you suspect is the victim—this Samantha—is, or was, a guest at the hotel where you are staying?"

"Yes, she was there when we arrived two days ago. Harriet could tell you when she checked in. And her last name," Whitt continued, as the door opened and another uniformed officer came in with a tray holding a teapot and cups.

"And who is this Harriet person?" The inspector asked, his brows starting to furrow. He seemed upset, as if the addition of players, meaning the more people that he had to interview, annoyed him. *Maybe he is hoping for an open-and-shut case, but accident victims don't hide themselves under heavy machinery.*

Finley considered what was bothering the inspector most—that a body had been found, that it looked like murder, that it was a foreign national, or that someone had gone to a lot of trouble to hide the body. What she wondered was how Samantha had been killed. The lack of blood had her stymied. She was also curious about how long the body had been there.

"Harriet Dissanayake. She's the owner of the Sandford House," Finley said.

"A local woman?" The inspector's lips pursed slightly, his eyes questioning.

"She's British and was married to a Sri Lankan gentleman," Whitt offered. "She's been here over ten years, as I recall."

The inspector seemed to relax, his brows unknitting and his lips moving from their previous tight purse.

"When did you last see this Samantha?"

"Yesterday afternoon. We went up to the overseer's watch and think we saw her there," Finley said.

"Both of you saw her? Was she near the watch point?"

"No, she was some ways away. I was looking through my camera's telephoto lens, and my sister had the binoculars," Finley said.

"What made you think it was this woman, given that you were far away?"

"It was the dress she was wearing," Whitt said. "It was a blue, A-line maxi with tiny white flowers on it. It looked so English countryside to me. I had made a remark about it earlier in the day. She was wearing it with a matching knit duster and soft-suede boots."

"And you could see all of that from your vantage point at the overseer's watch?" The inspector was trying to keep his expression neutral, but the tone of his voice suggested that he had doubts about Whitt's ability to see this level of detail.

"It wasn't just the blue and white of the dress, but the unique color of blue—a sapphire or cobalt—and the distinctive white sailor collar on the back. She had pulled the collar over the sweater, so the contrast was stark." Whitt paused, "There aren't many dresses with those details around here. And that can be seen from a considerable distance."

Whitt was starting to dislike this man. He was trying to dismiss her observations because they related to clothes and fashion. *Unless she was naked, which it didn't seem like she was, all you have to do is match this description to what she had on. It isn't rocket science.*

"And what time was it that you saw her?"

"Maybe two-thirty or three o'clock. It was before tea," Finley replied. She was watching Whitt closely. She could tell that the last exchange had miffed her. Before Whitt exploded on the inspector and got them both thrown in jail, Finley figured she should deflect her sister's anger.

"Was she at tea?"

"No."

"And was she at dinner?" The inspector paused, "Were you?"

"She wasn't at dinner, but we were," Whitt responded this time.

"Was it possible that she got a tray sent to her room?"

"Possibly. You would have to ask Harriet," Whitt said.

The inspector looked over at the young policemen, who was furiously writing copious notes using symbols that Whitt did not recognize.

"Can you tell me who the other guests are at the Sandford?"

"Besides Samantha, there was us," Finley responded.

"And Tom and the Lockes," Whitt added. "It is a small place. Just four rooms."

"Anything else you can tell me?" The inspector looked from Finley to Whitt. His eyes rested on Whitt for a moment before he turned to the policeman who was scribing. "Did you get all of that?" The young man nodded.

The inspector rose from his chair. "Then, I suppose, that is all for now, ladies. Please do not leave the area without letting us know."

Whitt and Finley stood and headed toward the door. Whitt was almost out the door before she remembered something. "Oh, you never asked whether Samantha was with anyone."

"Well, was she?" The inspector was a little agitated with the way Whitt phrased the statement. She was toying with him, she had to admit.

"She wasn't really with them, but I saw her, and I also saw the Lockes from the overseer's watch." Whitt had come back into the room and stood facing the inspector, a small upturn on her lip. "She was walking some distance behind them."

"Why did you not say this before? Was she following them?" The inspector's eyes narrowed. His little mustache twitched as if it was single-handedly holding back an outburst that the inspector was trying to stifle. The young scribe looked back and forth between his superior and Whitt, unsure of what would come next.

"Were they talking or engaging in any way?"

"Not that I could tell. The Lockes were walking, and Samantha was a fair distance behind them. It didn't appear that they even knew she was there."

"But she could see them."

"Yes, but what reason would she have to follow them? They both were just out on walks in the same area," Whitt said. "It would be a stretch to think otherwise. There were several people walking along the paths yesterday once the sun came out."

"Did you know any of them?"

"By sight, yes. We all bump into each other on these tours, and then see each other on the paths." Finley had reentered and stood just inside the door. "Several of the same people were at the tea factory today. There's only so much to do here, so we are bound to run into each other. I agree with Whitt. It means little."

The inspector had resumed his seat, his fingers steepled as he considered what the sisters had said. "Very well. Don't leave the area. And let the Lockes know we wish to talk to them tomorrow."

Finley and Whitt were almost to the car before either said anything. It was Whitt who spoke first, "Strange little man!"

The mood at Sandford House was somber. Tom and the Lockes were sitting in the front room when Finley and Whitt walked in. Tea was long over, and dinner was a couple of hours away. Harriet, hearing the car, had hurried to the door.

"You poor dears! Where did they take you? Helen said the police officer took you off without any explanation." Harriet was red faced and beads of perspiration collected on the faint hairs of her upper lip. "I was getting ready to call the British embassy, but then I realized you were American."

"No need for you to be worried, but thanks for the concern, nonetheless," Finley said.

"They just wanted to ask us some questions about Samantha and when we last saw her," Whitt added. "They'll want to talk to everyone who is a guest here. And probably everyone on the tour."

"I don't think they have any suspects," Finley said.

"Suspects?" Tom was on his feet now. "This wasn't an accident? And it was Samantha, you say?"

"Yes, sadly, it was Samantha. And it's hard to believe it was an accident when the body was found in a compartment under the machine and not inside it." Finley had moved to the fireplace, warming herself on the fire. It wasn't that it was particularly cold. She was chilled from the inside out. A dampness in her soul that she couldn't shake. *Who would want to kill that poor woman? She seemed so nice. Flighty, but nice.*

"Goodness! How did you find all that out?" Helen asked.

"I could see the machines where they found the body. It looked like she was hidden inside one of them in the cabinet-like casing that the big dryers have underneath," Finley said.

"I thought it was an accident when Helen described it," Tom said. "I just wonder what prompted her to go wandering off. And what could she have seen in a tea factory to have gotten herself killed?"

Finley looked at the assembled group. She wanted to talk about the lack of blood and her supposition that she might have been killed elsewhere and hidden there. But any one of these people could be the murderer. She realized how little she knew about them. The Lockes had been at dinner, but Tom hadn't. But then again, the Lockes had lied about being on the trails yesterday afternoon. It all depended on when Samantha had died, and that was hard to tell from what little Finley had seen.

"I think I need a washup and a drink!" Finley said. Whitt picked up on the signal and followed her back to their room.

"What are you thinking—besides this not being Murder Game anymore? This is for real," Whitt said.

"I don't know what to think. The Lockes lied. Tom wasn't at dinner last night, and neither was Samantha. There wasn't any blood where she was found or on the body." Finley turned to Whitt who had kicked off her walking shoes and sat on the bed rubbing life back into her feet. "Did you see any on the sheet when the gurney passed?"

63

"Quite honestly, just as I was going to look for blood, you gasped, and all my attention turned to you."

"Sorry. But that bracelet was such a surprise."

"So, what does no blood mean?"

"I don't know for sure, but generally, it would suggest that Samantha wasn't killed at the factory. My guess is that her body was just stashed there," Finley said. "But then why there? Because the person works there? Or for convenience?"

"Well, this is no more than cocktail conversation. We cannot get involved. That little inspector would love to throw me in jail." Whitt's lip curled at the mention of the man.

"I really do need a drink." Finley had emerged from the bathroom, having washed her hands and braided her hair away from her face. She was starting to rethink this long hair idea. She knew that Max loved her hair long, but she rather welcomed the convenience of her old pixie cut.

"Then let's go. I'm sure Harriet can find us something smooth and strong."

Harriet, anticipating their needs, had put a bottle of Balvenie 14 Caribbean Cask on the table. "Unless you would prefer something else?" she asked as they walked in.

Their eyes lasered in on the bottle. "That will do just fine," Whitt confirmed.

They had settled on the sofa by the fireplace while Harriet went to get some lowball glasses. Tom had apparently retired to his room. The Lockes sat on the chairs that faced the picture window, deep in hushed conversation. Helen looked up after a while.

"Was the interrogation difficult?" Helen's brows were knitted together, her eyes imploring.

"She's hated police stations since our boy died. They claimed we had something to do with his death." Richard's voice was hard, tinged with bitterness. "Turns out it was meningitis."

Helen's eyes locked onto her husband's face, but her vacant stare suggested that her mind was somewhere else. Neither Whitt nor Finley knew what to say. It was Harriet's coming back with the glasses that brought Helen back to the present.

"Would you care for some?" Whitt asked both the Lockes and Harriet, who refused.

"I never got into whiskey," Helen said as she returned to her normal talkative self. "Richard, he doesn't drink much besides ales and beer. That's what we always get at the pub down the road from us. Our pints of ale. We can sit and spin yarns all night over that pint."

Whitt and Finley had just finished their second glass of Balvenie when Harriet called them in for dinner. She had brought the Lockes their beers and each group settled into quiet conversation before ordering. The selection tonight was a chicken stew of some sort and grilled fish. As usual, Finley and Whitt ordered one of each and prepared to finish off the last of the previous night's chenin blanc. The sisters had just put in their order when Helen returned to the topic of the investigation.

"Is everyone going to be interviewed? That seems a bit excessive," she said. "It's probably a robbery gone bad. Why do they have to involve us?"

"I'm sure it's just procedural. They want to be sure that they have everyone's statement," Whitt said. "Nothing to worry about."

Whitt and Finley exchanged a glance. Finley wondered what Helen would say when the inspector told them that he had a witness placing them on a walk that the Lockes claimed never took place. Why had she even bothered to lie about something seemingly so insignificant? She couldn't imagine that either Helen or Richard had anything to do with Samantha's death. Why would they? They didn't appear to know each other outside of the context of the guesthouse.

The sisters could barely wait to finish dinner and retreat to their room. Whitt was the first to brush her teeth and hop into bed.

"Hurry up! We need to talk about the Lockes." She had pulled a book from her satchel, but it was clear that she had no intention of reading it.

Finley wiped makeup off her face with an Olay towelette, dropping the mascara-soiled sheet in the trash before she cut the bathroom light and slid into bed.

"Something *is* strange with those two."

"Yeah. But I guess losing a child would make you strange."

"Maybe, but—"

Before Finley could finish her observation, they heard high-
pitched, animal-like screams coming from another room. Whitt
threw on her robe and slippers and headed toward the door. When
she rounded the corner and headed into the corridor, she saw that
the door to the Lockes' room was open, and the screams had trans-
formed into shrill, unintelligible chatter.

Finley was close on her heels when Whitt knocked perfuncto-
rily on the door before barging into see what the ruckus was about.
Finley feared that Helen, overwrought by the prospect of a police
interrogation, had had a bout of hysterics. But that wasn't what was
making all the noise.

Helen stood in the center of the room with Richard slightly to
her right. She was squaring off against a rather large monkey that
appeared to be quite upset about something. Every time Richard
attempted to approach, presumably to shoo it out, the shrill screams
and pounding started back up. The window on one side was partially
open, explaining how it got in, but it didn't explain why it didn't
want to leave. The window opening was large enough to provide a
ready exit.

"Get the key before that thing runs off with the whole key ring!"
Helen screamed.

"I don't care!" Richard tried again to show the animal the way
to the exit, but his attempts were rebuffed with piercing shrieks. "If
he wants it, let him have it."

"But you can't let him have your drive."

Richard paused for a moment, considered what Helen had said,
and tried again to retrieve what appeared to be his key ring from the
floor. However, with each approach, the monkey furiously pounded

the rug and threw up its arms in reproach. It wasn't clear what the source of its frustration was.

"Have you figured out what it wants?" Whitt asked, staring in fascination at the furry brown creature throwing a tantrum like a two-year-old.

"When we came back from dinner, we found the monkey," Helen said. "He was trying to steal Richard's key ring. Richard had left it on the desk."

Finley looked around at the shredded paper and tossed books that had fallen to the floor around the desk. *Monkeys must like ripping up things. Looks like our room in Kandy. Messy little creatures.*

"Do you think if we go outside and open the window wider, he might get the message?" Whitt asked.

"I don't know. I don't know what he wants," Helen was close to tears. "I just want it to go away."

Richard nodded to Whitt, and Finley followed her outside. They moved in the darkness to the far side of the house, listening for the sound of monkey chatter. When they reached the window, Finley reached over a large bush to pull the window further open. Out of the corner of her eye, she saw a flicker of light, heard what she thought was a whistle, and moved aside just in time to avoid colliding with the fleeing monkey.

Richard's head came through the window just then.

"Thanks. That seemed to have done the trick."

"Did he get your key ring?" Whitt asked.

"No. He actually dropped it and took off," he said. "Strange. It was like he just lost interest in it."

Finley pushed the window closed and followed Whitt back around the corner of the house. She looked back to see if she saw the light again, but nothing was there.

"Did you see anything when we were around the other side of the house?" Finley asked Whitt.

"No, but I thought I heard something. When I listened again, I didn't hear it anymore," Whitt said. "Like a whistle."

They were now in the hall. Finley turned to Whitt and whispered, "I heard it, too."

"Something's not right."

"You can say that again."

Richard had stepped into the corridor. Helen hid herself behind him, clutching his arm as if he would protect her from whatever had unleashed the monkey on her.

"Thank you again, ladies," he said. "That was a bit unnerving."

"I know I locked that window," Helen said in a small voice that made her seem childlike and vulnerable. Richard turned and put his arm around her.

"It's all right, dear. The monkey's gone. No harm done," he said. "You just need some sleep."

"I think we all need sleep," Finley said. "Goodnight."

Once in their room, Whitt asked pointedly, "*What* in tarnation just happened?"

"I don't know, but we need to keep our eyes open. And stick together," Finley replied. "That wasn't a monkey. It was a chimp, and I don't think chimps are native to Sri Lanka."

7

AS PROMISED, **INSPECTOR PERERA CALLED** at the Sandford House to talk with Helen and Richard. He took the opportunity to talk with Tom and Harriet, as well. The inspector and the young officer, who served as his scribe, took over the study that Tom had been claiming as his office. The inspector spoke with the Lockes together first and then separately. The desperate look that Helen gave her husband as she walked into the room broke Finley's heart.

The police had asked all the guests and staff to stay in the guesthouse until the inspector left to make questioning easier. As soon as the inspector left, Tom went to change his flights. He had intended on heading to the airport later in the day, but the investigation threw a wrench in those plans. The inspector insisted that they stay in Nuwara Eliya until further notice. Harriet was gracious, and since she had no other guest vying for that room, she extended his reservation until… That was the question on everyone's mind. Until when?

"Where haven't we gone in this darling one-horse town?" Whitt was reviewing the guidebook to see if there were any other historical sites that they hadn't seen. "We haven't walked the Victoria Park or gone to the Golf Club. Do you think Ella would be off-limits? It's only an hour away from here."

Finley was switching the lens on her backup camera. Since she had taken those last shots of Samantha from the overseer's watch using the telephoto lens, she hadn't used this camera. She had backed up her pictures to the cloud, but she was a little wary of potentially losing the last images of Samantha alive.

"I don't think the inspector would think kindly of us running off to Ella. Let's head into town and see what else we can find there. Champagne at the Grand can always be our fallback."

"Let me change into something a little more presentable."

Finley knew that that involved ironing with Whitt. Between the ironing and redoing her hair, Finley had at least another forty-five minutes to play with her equipment before they would call for Adesh.

Whitt stuck her head out of the bathroom door. "Where do you think Tom was the evening before last? We didn't see him until late yesterday after we got back from talking with the inspector."

"Where did that come from?" Finley looked at her sister, who stood in the doorway with her toothbrush half out of her mouth.

Finley could hear running water and swishing before Whitt returned, wiping her mouth on a hand towel.

"I was just wondering," Whitt said. "I'm trying to fit the pieces together, and there're a lot of things that don't fit." She had finished ironing and was pulling an artfully embroidered silk tunic over her head to match with her off-white pants.

"You think he had something to do with this?"

"At this stage, everyone could have something to do with this. Except us, of course."

Whitt was talking to her sister through her reflection in the mirror. Finley had changed into dark linen pants and a peasant blouse. She offset the casualness of the outfit with a heavily jeweled

70

cuff and cabochon earrings. She slipped her feet into patent mules as she spoke.

"You've got that right."

Finley's mind ran to the people in the guesthouse—Tom, the Lockes, even Harriet. And then the tourists along the path, and the people wandering around the tea factory. She wondered how many other tours Newton's had done that day. If the inspector wanted to be thorough, he was going to have to talk to everyone near the tea factory between the time when Finley and Whitt saw Samantha on the path and when her body was discovered. Visitors and staff.

Whitt had picked up her satchel and was heading toward the door. She stopped and looked back at Finley who was following her.

"What?" Finley said.

"I still have not been able to make any sense of the monkey business last night. Have you?"

"No. The monkey—or chimp, should I say—was intent on doing something. I thought it wanted the key ring, but then Richard said it left without taking it."

"Helen looked petrified. I don't think she is all there."

Adesh navigated the road into Nuwara Eliya, his hand out of the window tapping a beat on the outside of the car, his head tilted as if he could have done the trip with his eyes closed. Whitt empathized with his ennui. She was ready to head to Udawalawe—anywhere but here.

"How long do you think they're going to keep us here?"

Finley had just asked Adesh to take them to the Golf Club. While she liked the Grand, she was ready to look at something new, however limited that newness was. Local people from the region were proud of their golf club, so she figured they might as well see what all the fuss was about.

"With you, I suspect the inspector will say forty years. You and he got off to a bad start."

"That aside, what do you think? I need to contact the hotels if we're going to be delayed," Whitt frowned. "Have you called Max?"

"I sent him a text with some of the details. He was funny. Said we keep finding dead bodies whenever we are together."

Whitt laughed uneasily, and then thought of their trip to Tangier the previous year. Two people had died at the hand of a man who had secrets that he wanted to hide. He had been willing to kill for them to stay hidden. Finley and Whitt had helped local police and Interpol not only find the killers, but also shut down a passport-fraud and human-trafficking operation. But the assistance had put their lives in danger several times, and neither sister was interested in repeating that adventure.

"The guidebook says the golf course is one of the oldest in the world. Definitely in Asia," Whitt had spread open the book to show Finley the manicured greens and rolling landscape into which the course had been fit. "The planters didn't have too bad a life."

"No, as long as some disease didn't wipe out your crop, snakes didn't bite your kid, and the price of tea stayed high enough for you to support your family while far away from any kith and kin that might offer a safety net."

Whitt turned in her seat and stared at her sister. "Buzz kill." Both Adesh and Finley smiled.

The club was a single-story colonial building, a much bigger version of the traditional planter's houses that populated the town alongside the more ornate mansions. Whitt and Finley walked through the steepled, wide-planked foyer toward the back of the building where a massive room with wooden beams, wooden floors, and wooden walls looked out onto the lush emerald and sea greens of the course. *Mama would like this. And Daddy would be in hog heaven with these fairways.*

A waiter escorted the two women to a couple of leather barrel chairs near the window. There were a dozen or so people scattered about the bar area, which was carpeted with worn Oriental rugs, no doubt brought from the Empire by planters and left behind when they departed or died. Finley saw people she recognized, but no one she knew. Nonetheless, she nodded in the direction of a few of the couples who raised their heads to acknowledge their entrance.

"More retired German tourists," Whitt scrunched up her face as if to block out an unpleasant smell that threatened to become an unpleasant taste. "Why do they travel in clumps?"

"I think it's more an age thing than a cultural one," Finely replied. She was thinking of the similar cliquishness of older Japanese and Chinese tourists. She thought through different nationalities and remembered that she rarely saw Spanish or Italian tourists overseas in big clumps. The Brits had tour-bus trips, but mainly in the UK. The French didn't seem to like clumping, and the Americans did all their clumping in the US for the most part these days. Gone were the days of the huge American tour groups of retirees with their gaudy Hawaiian shirts and loud comments.

"And I think we're latching onto stereotypes. Just because the only tour groups we've seen have been German doesn't mean all Germans clump."

"Whatever. As long as they aren't clumping in my hotel or guesthouse, I'm fine."

Finley smiled. Once her sister disliked something, she disliked it for a while. There was no point arguing. "What are you drinking?"

"Want to get a bottle? We always regret not getting the bottle after we are halfway through our second or third glass."

"True. What do you want: Pol or Veuve? They appear to have both."

"Pol." Whitt's answer was unequivocal. She was particular about her champagne. She would drink Veuve, one of Finley's favorites, but they had several that ranked higher on her list of preferences. One of those was Pol Roger. She and Churchill would have been fast friends.

73

"Done." Finley signaled for the waiter. "We have nowhere to go, nothing to do, and someone to drive. Shall we ask him to ice two?"

Whitt pretended to look shocked and then simply nodded. "Want something to nosh?"

"Shall we try their samosas and maybe their devilled chickpeas?"

With drinks and snacks ordered, Finley looked up to see a couple that had also been part of one of the German tour-bus groups heading toward their table. They were shown to a small table and settee beside the sisters.

"Hello, we seem to all have the same idea." The woman was tall, slender, and blond with watery blue eyes. She was dressed impeccably in perfectly fitting navy pants and a long-sleeved mariner's T. She opened the conversation. Finley couldn't place her accent. "Nothing much to do once you have toured and walked."

Finley nodded in agreement. It was the boredom of being in a place one day too long. No matter how creative you tried to get, the desire to move on was always there and colored everything you did.

"Have you been restricted to the barracks, too?" Whitt couldn't say why she had decided to use a military analogy, but the woman's companion, presumably her husband, laughed in response.

"I think the inspector has all foreign nationals in Nuwara Eliya under watch."

The man was disarmingly handsome with dark-brown hair, soft doe eyes, and an inviting smile that revealed exceptionally white teeth. Whitt knew her eyes had lingered on this face a bit too long, but she couldn't pull away. The man must have noticed. He stood and offered his hand.

"Alfred van Dijk," his lips curled slightly upward as he spoke. He knew he was attractive and was used to the effect it had on women.

Whitt recovered enough to speak, "Whitt Blake. And this is my sister, Finley."

"This is my wife, Lena." The woman smiled. She, too, was used to women's reactions to her husband. "Where are you from?"

"The States," Finley said. "And you?"

"Netherlands."

"Where in the Netherlands? I spent some time in Amsterdam."

"Haarlem. So, not far from the city. But I was born and raised in Amsterdam."

They continued on with light banter until the van Dijks' drinks and food came, and then each couple returned to private conversations as the afternoon slipped by.

Sometime later, when the van Dijks stood to leave, Alfred turned to Whitt and Finley. "Pleasure speaking with you. Will you be long in Sri Lanka?"

Whitt answered, "Another ten days or so. We're heading to Galle by way of Udawalawe. And you?"

"We'll head to Galle as soon as the inspector lets us go," Alfred said. "Perhaps, we will see you in Galle."

He stood aside and let his wife precede him. She nodded and then headed toward the other couples in the bar whom she apparently knew. Her husband followed and stood as his wife exchanged greetings with a few before taking their leave.

"Well, you were certainly taken with him," Finley teased. "Flirting with the man in front of his wife!"

"I wasn't. He just has an arresting allure. It was a little unsettling to have those eyes lock on you like that."

Finley smirked. *Give that girl champagne and the man-killer in her comes out. His wife seemed more amused than upset. Must get used to it with a guy that looks like that.*

Whitt had signaled the waiter. He moved silently to take the empty champagne bottle away and open the second bottle of Pol. He filled Whitt's glass and started to pour for Finley.

She hoped the inspector would release them so they could continue their tour of the island. Too many more days like this and she feared she and her sister both would become hopeless drunkards. She imagined many a planter's wife taking nips from her husband's liquor cabinet to stave off the utter boredom that came from seeing the same people do the same things day after day, year after year.

75

"They seem to have lost their lisping *s* in all that traveling they did while he was a banker." Finley continued in response to Whitt's quizzical look. "Amsterdamers have a slight lisp when they speak Dutch. Like Texans speaking English. It's subtle, but I can generally spot it."

"They didn't have it?"

"Not that I could tell when I overheard them. They could be from somewhere else originally and just claim Amsterdam as home."

"That's likely it. We have a lot of nerve talking about claiming places, though." Whitt reminded her sister of their own peripatetic lifestyle and the hesitancy it brought when anyone asked where they were from.

"And did you see his key ring?" Finley paused to take a sip of her bubbly as she waited for her sister's answer.

"Yeah. It looked just like Richard's. You don't see many rings that look like that. Maybe the van Dijks gave it to him. They seem like the friendly sort of rich people that give away stuff when it is admired."

"Then I should have mentioned the mega sapphire his wife had on her hand! She might have gifted it to me."

"And I should have been more vocal in my admiration of her husband. She might have handed over the leash."

"She did seem like the one in control, didn't she? Odd dynamic," Finley said. "But that would have only postponed the decision you have to make about David. Or have you forgotten?"

Whitt looked up at Finley and then lowered her eyes to stare into her champagne. "Don't remind me."

8

SANDFORD HOUSE WAS ABUZZ WHEN Whitt and Finley walked in the front door. The Lockes were seated side by side on the living room sofa having an animated conversation. Tom had staked claim of one of the easy chairs in the corner. Book in hand, his eyes were fixed on the Lockes.

"The inspector says we can go." Helen had jumped up from the living room sofa and grabbed Whitt by the arm. "We're getting out of here as soon as we can."

"He says we can't leave the island yet, though, so I think I am going to stay right here. As long as Harriet lets me," Tom broke in. His eyes diverted to Harriet, who was standing inside the hallway door, dish towel in hand. She smiled at him sweetly and then announced that dinner would be ready in an hour.

Finley and Whitt headed to their room to clean up and change for dinner. The Sandford wasn't a stuffy place, but if this was to be their last night, the sisters felt obliged to make some effort to dress nicely.

"So, it seems Tom is sweet on Harriet," Finley said, dropping her bag on the desk. "I didn't see that coming, did you?"

"Yes. I caught him holding her hand in the kitchen the day before yesterday. I thought it was because of Samantha, but I guess there was more to it."

"They are kind of cute together. Both soft and doughy."

"You are a snarky one."

"Me? You're the one that asked just yesterday if he was Samantha's killer. And today you're playing matchmaker. What's with that? You think they're in on it together?"

Finley had slipped off her pants and changed into a black linen shift dress with oversized, embroidered beige paisleys.

"Oh, I don't know what I think." Whitt was changing her earrings and studying her sister in the mirror. "It is strange that he was out of sight for much of the time in question. But then again, he's so sweet."

"It's the sweet ones that catch you off guard. Remember Peter?" Finley shuddered as she spoke the name of the charming actor-slash-production technician they had met in Morocco. He was the one who had brutally murdered two people. And he was the last person anyone had suspected.

"I know. But I'm hoping for Harriet's sake that he isn't involved. I think she likes him too."

Harriet had been married to a Sri Lankan man in London. They had been together for almost twenty years when they divorced. They had always planned to run a bed-and-breakfast in Sri Lanka when they retired. Despite their split, Harriet wasn't ready to give up on that dream. She had moved to Nuwara Eliya, bought the guesthouse, and managed it for ten years by herself. She deserved a bit of happiness.

"Well, let's hope it all works out for them and that they quickly catch whoever killed poor Samantha." Finley had grabbed her shawl and was heading for the door. "We forgot to ask if the police had any suspects. Helen will surely know."

Helen did know. She shared with Whitt and Finley all the information she had gathered from her talk with the police. Richard sat and listened quietly. Tom's head was stuck in his book. He looked up only when Harriet brought his dinner, smiling and letting his eyes follow her as she went about her duties, taking orders and serving drinks.

The offerings for dinner were a chicken curry and candied shrimp with curry rice. Since both had had the chicken before, the sisters doubled down on the shrimp and were glad for it when it came. The curry marinade, which included grated coconut, had been massaged deep into the shrimp flesh so that every part of the shell and meat was replete with the spices. Harriet and the chef had paired the blackened shrimp with slices of grilled, ball-shaped eggplant served over rice.

"This is divine." Finley had taken her first bite of the rice and eggplant.

"Wait until you taste the shrimp. I have to ask Harriet how they prepared this."

Finley's eyes closed as she savored the shrimp in the rich, savory sauce. "Damn, this is good. I wonder why she saved this for last."

"Agreed. I would've been ordering this every night if it had been on the menu."

"Helen, did the inspector come here to tell us that we could leave?" Finley brought herself out of her food stupor and turned to Helen, who was sitting at a nearby table.

"No, he sent one of his sergeants. The sergeant said that they had a suspect under arrest so we could go. They wanted us to stay on the island for another few days so that they could find us if they had questions. After that, we could leave the country if we wanted."

"Is that what you plan to do?" Whitt was sipping on a dry rosé. She peered over her glass, curious about what the Lockes were going to do. Helen had been so worked up about the monkey that Whitt was sure she would want to go home.

"No, we aren't leaving until we see all that we want to see," Helen was looking at Richard as she spoke, looking for assurance or approval. Whitt couldn't tell which. "It's scary, to be sure. Having someone you know killed."

"We're heading down to Galle. That was the plan originally," Richard said. "I guess we'll stick to it. And you? Where're you going to go next?"

"Udawalawe, for the elephants," Finley replied. "Then on to Galle for a bit."

"We had debated about going to the reserve. Maybe we'll go." Helen looked again at Richard. His face was neutral, but his eyes narrowed slightly when she suggested that they head to the elephant preserve. Finley wondered why it would matter.

"Do you know of good places to stay?" Helen asked. "I know it is the off-season, but everything still feels so crowded, and we don't like big hotels."

"We generally find places on Agoda. They tend to be smaller, less touristy," Whitt offered.

"That's what we like, too." Helen pushed her plate back and stood to leave. "Maybe we'll see you around. We're leaving here tomorrow morning, early." Richard grabbed his key from the table. Finley looked to see if he still had the unusual key ring, but all she saw was the key and no ring.

"'Night. And safe travels," Whitt called as they headed down the hall. Tom had left the room earlier, so it was just Finley and Whitt in the dining room.

"You were looking for the ring, too?"

"Yep. Maybe they took the key off the ring since they were getting ready to leave and didn't want to forget it."

"Maybe." Finley was staring into her wine, her long legs stretched out under the table. "It isn't our business in any case. So, what's the plan now?"

"You mean now that we can split Nuwara Eliya?" Whitt topped off her sister's glass and then poured herself more rosé. They needed to finish the bottle anyway. "We'll leave here tomorrow after lunch, like we planned, and head to the park. It'll take just under three hours."

"Good deal. No rush in any case. Are we going on a tour or do we have a driver for the park?"

"The guesthouse said they would arrange it."

Whitt pushed back from the table and carried her wine into the living area where Harriet had lit a small fire. The night was nippy again, and the fire's warmth made a pleasant ending to a rather mundane day. Finley had followed her into the room but stood with her head turned toward the hall. She put her finger to her lips. Whitt strained to hear what had caught her sister's attention.

Finley signaled Whitt to join her. Putting her wine on the table, Whitt quietly walked over to stand in the door.

"So... To Galle as soon as possible." They could hear snatches of a conversation in Helen's voice, which was now pitching higher and louder, as if she were upset. "But that doesn't mean we can't go to the park."

"Helen, we're already... Samantha delayed us..." Richard's end of the conversation went in and out as he modulated his resonant voice.

"But I want to go!" Helen was getting more agitated. After a while, she appeared to be sobbing. They could hear nothing more from Richard.

Whitt returned to her wine, and Finley took a seat beside her. "What was that about?" Finley said.

"Don't know. I told you she isn't all there."

Finley and Whitt arrived at the game park just before four o'clock. The sun was harsh in its warmth, making the contrast from Nuwara Eliya's cooler clime even starker. The hotel was little more than individual tree houses nestled around a center clubhouse. Each stilted hut was equipped with a small kitchen area with a mini-fridge and a microwave.

"Not a bad setup." Whitt had walked through the room, running her hand over the pillows and sheets, inspecting the towels, and looking at the shower stall.

"What were you expecting to find? What's with the pat-down of the beds?"

"You can tell a lot from the feel of the sheets." Whitt had sat down on one of the camp chairs that graced the platform patio outside the main room. From that vantage, she could see the top of the canopy and see the movement of branches as nearby elephants made their presence known.

Finley's puzzled look prompted Whitt to continue. "First off, you can feel if there are any nasties—like snakes or scorpions—under the sheets before you put your feet in. Then, you can tell the quality of the place by how soft the sheets and towels are. I like soft sheets and towels."

Finley smiled. *That's not all you like. You are high maintenance personified, girl.*

"And I like a clean, well-maintained bathroom. After all the *basic*—and I use that term loosely—guesthouses and rooms that I've stayed in out in the field, when I pay for it, I like it clean." Whitt turned to look at her sister, who had joined her in the chair beside her.

"I can't disagree with that," Finley said. "Does this meet your requirements, ma'am?"

Whitt nodded. "We'll see whether the rest of the amenities measure up."

The night passed without event. The Land Rover with the driver and the guide arrived the next morning in pristine condition and on time—and with water bottles for each guest and a cooling towel after the dusty ride into the park proper. Whitt was satisfied that the safari lodge met her standards. The Rover was an open-sided vehicle with a center aisle and seating for eight people. When the car arrived to pick them up, there was only a young man in his mid-twenties in the vehicle.

"Hello, I guess we're going to be partners in crime today!" he said as Finley and Whitt climbed in and got settled.

Finley had brought her telephoto lens, as well as another camera and a satchel full of filters. She wasn't sure what the dust would do to the clarity of her shots and wanted to be sure that she had what she needed to cut through the haze. As such, she had a couple of bags strapped across her that made moving around a bit cumbersome.

"Hope I didn't bop you when I got in. This equipment can be awkward sometimes." Finley extended her hand. "Finley Blake. And my sister, Whitt."

"Oliver McNair." He shook hands with both sisters. "Where are you from?"

"The States." Whitt had figured him to be a grad student from Washington state or Oregon, so she was surprised when he said he was an architect from Toronto.

"How long are you in Sri Lanka?" Whitt continued. Finley knew her sister could be like a pit bull after a bone when she was getting the real skivvy on someone. For some reason, this guy interested her. Before they returned to the hotel that night, Whitt would know his girlfriend's name and whether he was likely to marry her, as well as his greatest fears—besides marriage.

"Last few of my ten days here, and then off to the Maldives for diving."

While they bumped along the road that connected the hotels, lodges, and cottages, Whitt and Oliver talked about the diving conditions in a range of places from California to Palawan. Whitt wasn't a big diver, but she had her license and had gone numerous times with David, who knew most of the best places in the world for the sport.

They were so engrossed in the conversation that they didn't notice that the Rover had stopped, and the door had opened. During the ride between the hotels, Finley and Whitt had turned in their seats to face Oliver, who had claimed one of the back seats. Then, they heard an all-too-familiar voice. Before they saw her, they heard Helen's voice scolding Richard about sunscreen.

"Well, I'll be. We run into you again!" Helen seemed genuinely pleased to see the sisters. "And who is this dear boy?"

Oliver blushed. "Oliver McNair, ma'am. I take it you all know each other."

"We were all in the same hotel in Nuwara Eliya." Richard caught Helen's eye as if to warn her off talking too much. She understood his meaning and took the conversation in a different direction.

"Have you ever been on a safari before?" she asked. "This is my first time, and I'm so excited."

Shehan, the guide, explained the precautions necessary in an open vehicle once inside the park, given the diversity of wildlife they were likely to see—antelopes, water buffaloes, jackals, leopards, flamingoes, and of course, elephants.

As they rode around the reserve looking for animals, Whitt made Oliver the focus of the conversation, deftly cajoling him into revealing much of his past and a lot of his future aspirations. He was an engaging conversationalist, peppering his responses with amusing stories that cast him as a mama's boy living in the shadow of an older brother, who was an officer in the Canadian Navy and whom Oliver idolized.

While Oliver kept them laughing, spurred on by prods from Helen and Whitt, Finley focused her eyes and camera on the panorama. Even when there was no visible wildlife, the scenery was worthy of capture. She scanned the horizon for movement—wavering leaves, puffs of dust—and then instinctively moved her lens in that direction, waiting for the reveal.

She had been able to catch a mother and baby elephant duo grazing, a tree-load of pocket monkeys so populous that they looked like flowers on the tree branches, and by fluke, a leopard breaking cover to make for a napping tree. All the while, Richard sat face forward, saying little.

After several hours of touring, the group enjoyed a convivial lunch, munching on roti stuffed with either devilled chicken or jackfruit curry, which they topped off with a couple of bottles of rosé. They used the hood of the Rover as a table, covering it with a patterned tablecloth and spreading the fare on it.

Helen chatted with the group for a while before taking her roti and wine and joining Richard on the tailgate, which had been lowered to make a seat. Their conversation was difficult to hear, but Richard's body language spoke volumes. He didn't want to be there, regardless of what Helen wanted. He was not pleased.

The others in the group tried to make light of it, refocusing their attention on movement on the banks of the river as various animals came to drink. Anosh, the driver, had parked them on a promontory that overlooked the river but put them in no danger with the animals venturing to the watering hole.

By the time the group made use of the facilities not far from the lunch site, Shehan and Anosh had packed up the picnic basket and cleared the area of any debris. Shehan pulled perfumed, moistened towels from the cooler and passed them around. The clean smell of citronella and lime revitalized Finley and Whitt. They were fueled and ready for the next adventure.

Shortly after lunch, Shehan received a call from another member of his scouting team, alerting them to a possible leopard sighting. Not far from where Finley had caught sight of the leopard scaling the tree, a guide had come upon another two leopards, a large male and a smaller female, who were treed and sleeping lazily. They were presumed to be mates since this was generally the only time that these solitary animals came together.

Anosh took off at breakneck speed, sending a cloud of red dust flying behind the car. As the Rover came around a curve in the road, he slammed on the brakes. There, in the road, was a caravan of elephants, some ten to fifteen females with their young in tow. The herd ambled across the road, seemingly unconcerned with the car or its passengers. Occasionally, one of the females would encourage one of the young that had slowed with a gentle nudge from behind.

Finley watched in awe as the group paraded across the way. She switched her shutter to silent to reduce the distraction of the clicking sound and took frame after frame of the group as it made its way toward the river. She had just switched lenses and was adjusting a filter when the trumpeting started. She froze. She had heard that trumpeting could mean any number of things, but the volume and stridency of this trumpet seemed to suggest only one thing—anger.

Shehan slowly raised his hand to indicate that all motion was to cease. As the last of the herd reached the other side of the road, a mature female, perhaps the leader of the group, had come forward, ears outright, tail rigid, and trunk raised. She shook her head several times, stepping forward and then moving back as if uncertain whether a mock charge would be sufficient, or whether the threat was real enough to warrant an actual one.

Their guide had hoped that by going quiet and motionless, the female would see that the Rover and the people in it meant no harm. It seemed to work. The female stepped back, still shaking her head, but relaxing her tail slightly. She had backed into the group that had gathered into a tight circle and appeared to relax when a sudden popping noise rang out, followed by a cry of pain from somewhere within the herd.

In the split second that followed, Anosh had put the Rover in gear and floored it while Shehan had grabbed what appeared to be a rifle from the floor of the car. Richard grabbed Helen and pulled her head into his lap as he tried to take cover behind the seat. Oliver launched himself from his seat into Whitt's and wrapped his arm around her. Finley turned in her seat, anchoring her body with her knee and steadying her lens against the back of the seat. She flicked the shutter to automatic and concentrated on pointing the camera in the direction of the action.

The female responded to the apparent attack on the herd. Her tail immediately went rigid again. She tucked her trunk inward, and with frightening speed, thundered after the Rover. For a moment, she appeared to be gaining on the car. She lowered her head like a bull, preparing to use it to overturn the car. But in no time, the Rover pulled away from her, leaving her standing in the road, roaring in anger and frustration.

"Are you all OK?" Shehan's voice was loud above the Rover's engine, which was still in overdrive as Anosh put more distance between the herd and the car.

Oliver and Whitt nodded, both still entwined. Richard was stroking Helen's hair and talking to her softly as she quietly sobbed. Finley, still locked into a reverse position in her seat, was scanning the landscape with her camera.

The popping sound had come from her right, but the underbrush was too dense to see anything clearly. She couldn't imagine a person being crazy enough to wait in a thicket without the benefit of a car or truck as defense, yet she had heard no engine other than the Rover's. And she hadn't seen anything besides bush and elephants. And if they were indeed waiting, what—or *who*—were they waiting for?

"I apologize for the drama back there," Shehan said. "I can't imagine what prompted her to charge us. I thought she was just trying to intimidate us. That is not unusual. But an actual attack…"

His voice trailed off as he shook his head, puzzled by the female's behavior. "Shall we continue to the leopards, or have you had enough for the day?"

Finley, Oliver, and Whitt waited for a response from Richard. It all depended on Helen. She was sitting up and had wiped her face of tears.

"Let's see if the leopards are still there," she said brightly. "I may never get a chance to see leopards again."

The group, surprised by Helen's quick recovery, looked at Richard. He appeared unfazed by the quick shifts in her mood. "The lady says she wants leopards. Let's see if we can find them."

After checking with his scout, Shehan directed Anosh to the area of the leopard sighting. While many of the Rovers had moved on after getting their requisite pictures of the wild cats, there were a few like their crew that were just arriving. The animals were dozing in the saddle of a large ironwood tree and seemed immune to all the fuss. Shehan unlatched the sunroof and rolled back the canvas so that Finley and the rest could stand on their seats to get a better view.

Whitt was depending on Finley to get some good shots. She hadn't even bothered to pull her iPad from her satchel. Oliver had climbed on the seat and was using his phone to capture some shots. Finley, for her part, was glad she had invested in the telephoto lens for just these sorts of situations.

"Send me some of those if you don't mind!" Oliver called over his shoulder, and then cheekily pointed at Whitt. "And one of her!"

Through the viewfinder, Finley had a clear view of the sleeping cats, their whiskers twitching to dislodge errant flies. She took her time, adjusting her angle slightly every now and then to catch brighter patches of light through the leaves, marveling at the leopard's ability to match his spots to the pattern of light that shone through the foliage. *Wait until we tell this story and show these to Max. He is going to be green with envy. But damn, David isn't going to like that somebody else was comforting his girl.*

9

THE TRIP TO GALLE HAD been uneventful. After the elephant charge, it was hard to find much else to equal the excitement. Adesh listened with concern to the story that Helen had richly embellished when he was dropping the sisters off at the hotel in Udawalawe. He had called to question both Shehan and Anosh, feeling responsible for Finley and Whitt while they were in his care. Their explanation had left him baffled but satisfied that there had been no negligence on the tour operator's part.

The Dutch House, their launch point in Galle, provided the quiet respite the sisters needed as they mulled over all the events of the past few days. Murder and mayhem were the sum of it. It would have made a good title for a book or theme for an ad campaign. But it wasn't what either sister had wanted for their vacation.

The hotel, situated in a residential area favored by many of the Dutch who still held property in Sri Lanka after its independence, was actually a cluster of residences that had been bought by a Londoner from a Dutch-Sri Lankan and turned into a boutique hotel. It sat on a tree-lined hill overlooking the port and the rest of Galle Fort. The location on high ground had proved fortuitous when the 2004 tsunami struck, washing away thousands who were going about their daily lives in the streets below.

"What's the plan while we are here?" Finley asked.

Finley lounged in the sitting room that adjoined their bedroom, looking out onto the manicured center courtyard. The hotel was U-shaped with the reception and lobby on one of the long sides, and the bedrooms, of which there were four, occupying the other two sides. A massive, tiered pool, surrounded by a garden, closed the rectangle. As compact of a blueprint as it was, it somehow felt spacious and never-ending: a lush oasis in the heart of the old city of Galle, with its narrow streets and winding alleyways.

"No real plan today. I thought we would just wander and get the lay of the land," Whitt replied.

"What does the guidebook say about the history? I recall some-thing about it being a vibrant Ptolemic trading post long ago."

"You have a good memory. It says here that it was listed on Ptolemy's world map as a port of call and was used by the Greeks, Chinese, Arabs, and others for trade," Whitt recounted.

Whitt had opened the large, wooden shutters that acted as a door at the foot of their spacious room before collapsing on the sofa opposite her sister with her book. With the doors thrown back, the room gave way to a view of the grounds and the two-level pool and fountain. A peacock strutted across the grass, unconcerned by Finley and Whitt's presence; this was its domain, and the humans were interlopers at best.

"I could get used to this." Finley stared out onto the expanse of green. "This country has every topography there is smashed into such a small space—beaches, hills, forests, jungles, deserts—OK, so maybe not deserts."

"I know," Whitt said, distractedly. It was clear from her expres-sion that she had heard only half of what Finley had said.

Whitt continued, reading from the book: "It says here that this room, the one we're staying in, was a favorite of Mick Jagger.

And Sting slept here, too!" Whitt probably wouldn't have given Mick the time of day, but she had always been kind of sweet on Sting, even now.

"Well, let's get going then. We can find lunch down the hill." Finely was up and had grabbed her satchel and sunglasses.

"Shall we ask what the options are for dinner?" Whitt said. "I didn't see a dining room anywhere."

At reception, Finley and Whitt were greeted by a distinguished gentleman with a shock of curly white hair. In his younger years, he would have been decidedly handsome. Now he looked like a kind but still attractive grandpa.

"Welcome, ladies! I hope you are getting settled. Heading down the hill?" he inquired.

"Yes. We thought we would wander today and do serious sight-seeing tomorrow. Any suggestions?" Whitt was eyeing the polo shirt he was wearing with interest.

"Have an interest in an elephant polo?" He smiled, seeing her eye rest on the logo of his shirt. "I'm Paul Druthers. I own this little gem and a few others on the island. Most importantly, I am the chair of the polo club here."

"Elephant polo?' Finley turned from looking at a Michael Ondaatje journal that had been nonchalantly dropped on a side table. It appeared from the insert in the back of the journal that Ondaatje, a Sri Lankan, had also stayed at the house at some point.

"Is there any other kind? It was invented here, although others claim it. We have a tournament next week. You should join us. It is great fun—hats and champagne. Like Ascot!"

"We'll have to see where we'll be, but please let us know the details," Whitt said. "By the way, is there a dining room here or is it best to get dinner in town?"

"You have a few options. We have a bar and dining room across the road at Cinnamon Gardens or we can set up meals on the ve-randa outside your rooms." He continued, "Then there are several nice restaurants down the hill." He offered them each a brochure that listed dining options in town.

"Whatever we decide, we will join you for cocktails at least," Finley said as she turned toward the door.

Finley caught up with Whitt who had slipped out of the door and headed toward the street.

"You're in a hurry."

"Nope, just didn't want to spend my day chewing the fat. We have things to do, places to see."

"And you have an appointment with either a jeweler or a dressmaker."

"A jeweler. How did you know?" Whitt turned to look at her sister.

"I know you," Finley smirked. "What stones are we looking for today?"

"I don't know for sure, but I think a sapphire."

"What color? Aren't there orange ones?"

"Yep, but I think I want a yellow or white one."

"Then let's get shopping."

The trip to the jeweler took less than forty minutes. Whitt had been referred by a colleague who had bought raw stones from this dealer before, finding him reputable and his prices reasonable. Whitt had looked at tray after tray of stones, even considering some more traditional, deep-blue Ceylon sapphires. In the end, she had settled on a large, clear, diamond-looking, cushion-cut stone and a smaller, emerald-cut, orange one. Finley, on a whim, bought two strands of cabochon moonstones, which she looped around her neck and wore out of the store.

"I like these. They go with everything. They look good with navy," Finley was pointing to the navy tunic Whitt was wearing. She then pressed a strand against the vibrant, burnt-orange T-shirt she had on. "Or this."

"Those were a good buy," Whitt said as she touched the moonstones. "Before we leave, I'm going to have to get a few strands. They're native to Sri Lanka."

"Well, right now, I need to go get coffee. We can decide lunch while we are sipping!"

They found a coffee shop not far from the palisades that encircled the fort city. Sri Lankan coffee, while not as famous as its teas, was still grown on the island in small quantities. Finley had taken a liking to the robusta blends that she had had in Colombo and had heard that Galle's European influence had inspired some of the best coffee shops in the country. As they sat down at one of the wrought-iron outdoor tables looking toward the lighthouse, they heard their names.

"Whitt!" Oliver McNair, Whitt's young Canadian protector from the elephant safari, was waving to them from the street. "Finley. Nice to see you."

"And you. If you aren't in a hurry, please join us. We were just grabbing coffee." Finley gave Whitt a side-glance and a half-smile. *Let's see if she blows the boy off or encourages him. Poor David. "Whitt uncertain" is "Whitt in a mood." And that can be really unpleasant.*

"When did you guys get in? I remember you saying you would get here at some point, but I didn't know when."

Whitt remained silent, so Finley jumped in to avoid an awkward pause in the conversation.

"Just this morning. We stayed an extra day in Udawalawe. Our driver must have scared the tour operator so much that they gave us another tour of the animal reserve on the house."

"Did you have the same driver and guide?"

"We did indeed. We felt bad. It wasn't their fault that the elephant charged. And it wasn't as if the tour was cut short," Finley continued.

Her sister sat drinking her coffee, still saying nothing. *Is she feeling guilty about falling into the boy's arms? Stonewalling him won't make it any easier talking to David about it. Or maybe she is just trying to nip it in the bud. Whatever she is doing is sure making it damn awkward for me.*

"Sri Lankan coffee is quite good. I am pleasantly surprised." Oliver appeared to be struggling to make polite conversation, too. "Are you a coffee or a tea drinker, Whitt?"

"Either, if it is good," Whitt cryptically replied. She disengaged, fixing her eyes on the lighthouse in the distance, coffee cup in hand.

"So where are you off to next, Oliver?" Finley tried gallantly to redirect the snub.

"Another day or so here and then to Colombo for the short flight to the Maldives. Can't wait to go diving." His face was eager with excitement. He reminded Finley of a puppy looking forward to its favorite bone.

Finley and Oliver talked briefly of the dives that they had done. Finley had just finished her training and had only gotten to do a couple of dives with Max. Whitt, on the other hand, had gone diving numerous times with David, a California boy who loved the sea and water adventures. *Why am I talking dives when it should be Whitt? What is with her blue funk? Hope she shakes out of it soon. I am not having my time in Galle ruined by her mood.*

Finley was so much in her own head that she hadn't noticed that Oliver had gotten up and was reaching for his wallet. She came around quickly.

"What are you doing? No need. This one is on us!" Finley said, waving her hand to get him to put his wallet away.

"You sure?" Oliver looked questioningly. "Then, next one's on me."

"Done. Have a great tour of Galle and an even better one in the Maldives."

"Thanks. I'll let you know how it goes." He hesitated, looking at his phone. "I think I have your contact info from the safari."

"I know we have yours. I owe you pictures," Finley said, smiling at the thought of his not-so-subtle request for a picture of Whitt. "I'll resend ours, just in case."

Oliver nodded and headed off toward the lighthouse and battlement walls. As soon as he was outside hearing distance, Finley turned to her sister.

"So, what's the deal? You trying to be invisible?"

"I just didn't have anything to say."

"So says Chatty Cathy with an attitude!"

Whitt said nothing. Her eyes were fixed on her coffee cup. When she raised them, Finley could see they were brimming with tears.

"OK, kid, what's going on? You have got to talk it out." *The pot's calling the kettle black! Since when have you ever talked anything out? For four years you kept your mouth shut about what had happened with Max.* Finley took in a breath. *But only because I didn't know. She knows.*

"I didn't mean to be rude. I'm so sorry." Whitt was crying now. Tears streamed down her face and she made no effort to stop them. "I miss David so much and I haven't heard from him. I'm scared. Scared that I've lost him."

"Would that be a bad thing? You said you needed space. He said he wanted marriage. That's close. Real close."

"I wanted space, not distance."

"Then tell him. He can't read your mind, baby sis. Have you talked to him?'

"No."

"Why not?"

"I didn't know what to say."

"Would 'I love you' have been too hard?"

"What if he didn't say it back?"

"He already said he did. You were the one that didn't answer."

"Oh, God. I've really lost him."

"You won't know until you talk to him."

"What time is it?"

Finley called the waiter for another cup of coffee while Whitt moved to another table and punched David's name on her phone. All Finley could hear above the noise in the café was "I love you." The rest was chatter.

When Whitt returned to the table, she was grinning like a Cheshire cat.

"All good?" Finley asked.

"All good," Whitt responded. "Do you mind if he comes down?"

"Nope. I'm just glad you both talked. I do need to get some gifts and you have a better nose for a good buy than I do, so let's get that done before he gets here."

The rest of the afternoon was spent wandering in and out of shops, picking up spices, grinders, coffees, and more teas. Finley bought a few pendants and bracelets with fragments of colored stones in them. The artisans claimed that they were pieces of semi-precious gems, but Finley suspected that it was more likely colored glass. It mattered not to her. She liked the designs and thought the recipients would appreciate the gifts, if for nothing more than the thought behind it.

Finley and Whitt both savored a long bath following their extensive walking and shopping jaunt. Whitt had bought some bath salts that were guaranteed to take the tired out of your bones, per the saleslady at an Ayurvedic shop. She figured that even if they didn't, they smelled nice.

"Are we staying in or going out for dinner?" Finley was the first one out of the bath and dressed. She had asked the front desk whether she could borrow the Ondaatje journal and sat thumbing through it. She was sure that much of *Running in the Family* had come from this journal.

"Let's go grab a drink and then decide."

They learned from the front desk that to get to the bar, they had to cross the narrow street—though it was more like an alley—and enter the barely marked gate. From there, they followed directions that took them through the garden onto the patio, through the small dining room and into a tented sunroom no bigger than a butler's pantry. In that space sat four other couples, gathered on floral-patterned banquettes, with their drinks in hand since there were no tables.

"Welcome again!" It was Paul. "Hope you had an enjoyable afternoon. What can I get you to drink?"

As Finley and Whitt gave him their drink order, the others introduced themselves. They were people that the sisters had seen in one of the tour groups on the island—the misnamed German tour group that included British, Dutch, and German travelers. They were all staying in the Gardens, which offered more traditional rooms with kitchenettes.

"Are you long in Sri Lanka?" asked one woman, whose name Finley had heard but managed to forget in the process of introductions. She wasn't sure whether the woman wanted to know how long they had been in the country or how long they were staying.

"We arrived a little over a week ago and will be staying for a little over another week." Finley replied. "And you?"

"Our tour was for ten days, so after tomorrow, we go to Colombo and then home."

"And where is home?" Whitt had joined the conversation now that she had her champagne. It wasn't a vintner that she knew, but the taste was good, and the bubbles were small and vibrant. "We are from Dusseldorf, as are our friends, the Liebners. The Hoffners are from Nuremburg and these people are Dutch, from Leiden." She pointed to the young couple who sat nearest Finley.

Paul came from behind the bar and leaned against the door jamb as introductions were being made. As the evening progressed, he proved himself to be a skilled conversationalist, prodding the discussion when it lagged with questions that prompted those gathered to share a perspective or an opinion. By the second bottle of champagne, a few plates of samosas and some curry-fried cashews, the Liebners and Hoffners had moved to a table for dinner, and the Dutch couple had called for a cab to take them into town for their dinner reservation.

"Let's just stay here and nosh," Whitt suggested, as the waiter began pouring from the second bottle.

"Fine with me. I don't think I want to move." Finley was looking at the polo jerseys and pictures on the wall. The decor looked like a mix of tack room mismatch and tearoom schmaltz. There were polo shirts, mallets, and award pictures mounted over white, garden-latticed walls with bold, floral-print curtains and cushion covers. As distracting as the furnishings were, the pictures themselves were mesmerizing. They shared a history of place and time.

"Are these all of you and your family?" Whitt asked Paul, who had returned after seating the Germans for dinner. He was pouring himself a whiskey from behind the bar.

"Yes. Family and some polo-playing friends. I've lived here and in the UK for ages." He stretched his legs out in front of him, using his body to divide the little room in two. "Played polo in England and got hooked on elephant polo when I moved here."

"Seems you are quite good at it. Do you have all of your trophies here or in England?"

"Bit here and there. I have another house on the island."

Whitt shifted the conversation. "By the way, is it possible to get another room for three or four days?"

"Are you tossing your sister out or adding another friend?" Paul knew that it was more likely that a friend was coming, and most probably, a gentleman, but he enjoyed making young ladies blush.

"A friend," was all Whitt volunteered.

"I am sure something can be arranged. Just let me know when he is arriving."

Whitt's eyebrow shot up. *I didn't say my friend was a guy. Cheeky.*

Paul smiled slyly and stood up. He placed his half-finished drink on the small bar counter.

"Enjoy your stay, ladies." He bowed slightly. "I will see you in the morning."

"CAN WE GO TO TEA at the Galle Fort today?" Finley asked.

She and Whitt were sitting on the veranda outside their room over breakfast the next morning. Whitt had opted for toast and fruit while Finley had an egg hopper. She was starting to get used to the texture of the hopper and now remembered to ask them to cook her egg a bit harder.

She listened to the chatter of the monkeys in the trees, knowing they were talking among themselves about the best tactic for snatching leftovers from the table for their breakfast. She knew, too, that the housekeepers, who sat on small stools outside the rooms, understood the monkeys' conversation well and were prepared to repel the little creatures when they came marauding.

Whitt had just taken a bite of toast with marmalade, so Finley continued while Whitt chewed.

"I know that once David comes, you're going to want to go with him, and I don't want to be a third wheel."

"Sure, I don't mind going twice if David does want to go. I suspect, though, that he will skip froufrou-y tea, so if I don't go with you, I won't get to go at all."

"Good. Now that that is settled, what else do you want to do? We can save Yala for all of us to do. And you can take him to whale watch."

"When do you want to do the turtle sanctuary?"

"We can decide after lunch. We don't have to cram too much in. This is a vacation, not a race. What time does he get in?"

"He said he would try to make it for dinner around seven o'clock or so. That gives us all day to tour. And can we look at another jeweler while we are out? Paul mentioned him in the guest materials, and the concierge said they had some interesting designs."

Finley smiled. She was glad to see that her sister's shopping spirit was back. If there was shopping to be done, Whitt and Mama were the ones to do it, unless they were in ill humor. That's when you were in for real trouble. With David coming, the storm had passed.

"No problem. Let's go."

The first stop was at the Dutch Reform Church inside the fort walls. Not only was the church architecture beautiful, but the cemetery also offered a poignant history of the city and the trials of its inhabitants.

Finley and Whitt had started the macabre practice of reading tombstones when they were children, traveling with their parents. While Mama and Daddy were on organized tours of ancient monuments and stately castles, Finley and Whitt were often sent outside to run around.

After discovering that first cemetery in Corsica, the one that had pictures of the buried in little frames on the headstone, the sisters were hooked. They could be found wandering around a graveyard, reading the ages of the buried and how they had wanted to be remembered.

"Good gracious, this whole family was lost. Three children and the mother. And then you find the father over here, a few years later."

"Looks like several families died at the same time." Finley had moved to another set of headstones grouped together. The cobble-stones underfoot were uneven from the ground settling beneath the stones. "Does it say what killed them? There's nothing here."

"Nope, we'll have to ask around."

"Or check the internet." Finley moved to look at a larger mau-soleum in the center of the rather austere graveyard. "What time is your meeting with the jeweler?"

"I set it for after lunch, so we didn't have to rush."

"What are you looking for this time?"

"Large moonstones. There's a mine nearby." Whitt's eyes bright-ened like a miner who had struck the motherload. "They say the best ones come from around here. Maybe we should do a tour."

"Well, before I do anything else, I need more coffee."

They headed toward a coffee shop not far from an artist enclave that had been established inside the fort. Both sides of the alleyway leading to the coffee shop were lined with industrial art, canvases, and sculptures by local and visiting artists. The few tourists that were around seemed to crowd into the narrow street, drawn by either the art or the coffee, whose smell was wafting up the street.

A face in the crowd caught Finley's eye, but before she could process what she saw, the person was gone. *I really do need coffee. I am seeing things. I could swear I saw Evans.* Two cups later, Finley finally broached the possibility with Whitt.

"I think I just saw Evans. Is that possible?"

Whitt pulled her sister's sunglasses off her nose, looked deep into her eyes, and shook her head.

"You are seemingly lucid, not under the influence of medica-tion—or excessive alcohol—and appear to have had enough coffee. So, yes, it is possible. But no, it is not likely."

"That's what I thought. I just wanted to confirm." She was quiet for a minute before she continued. "But last time I said I thought I saw someone, the camera confirmed it."

Finley was talking about their adventure in Morocco when her hunch about seeing someone had proven true and they ended up uncovering a sad and bloody saga.

Whitt sensed what Finley was thinking. She got up and pulled a tip for the busser out of her coin purse. "Well, have your camera ready next time."

The two spent the rest of the day touring the temples and museums in the old fort. They decided to skip lunch and have the full tea when teatime came. So, after the jewelers and more gift shopping, they headed to tea. The Galle Fort Hotel was the perfect venue for this sort of indulgence. The building had begun three centuries before as a Dutch merchant's mansion and had gone through multiple incarnations before being restored as a boutique hotel.

Finley and Whitt chose to be seated near the front windows that opened to the street. The dark-wood furniture and molding against the textured white of the walls and the satiny smoothness of the plantation shutters evoked a quiet elegance of an era lost.

Whitt sipped her champagne and indulged in what she said was her last smoked-salmon finger sandwich. In the last twenty-four hours, she had acquired a sense of inner peace that had been missing for most of the time the sisters had been in Sri Lanka.

"So, is he coming because you said yes or because he needs to convince you to say yes?" Finley was munching on a mini raspberry tart, her eyes fixed on her sister.

"We didn't even get to that. He's coming because he misses me as much as I miss him."

"If he had asked you, what would you have said?" Finley couldn't tell by Whitt's facial expression what emotions and questions were racing through her mind. She sensed that her sister had come to a decision, whether she was willing to admit it or not.

"I don't know. I think I would have asked a lot of the questions that need to be asked, but I don't know that the answer would have been so clear-cut."

"Will you marry me? Yes, or no?"

"If I can continue to travel, if we can live overseas, if it's OK if we don't have kids immediately, if I can keep working even after kids, if we can stay mental and emotional partners, if I don't ever have to live in California for more than two years—then yes, I will marry you."

Whitt's face lit up when she said the last four words. Finley wished that David had been there to see the transformation, the acquiescence, the deep affirmation of self that came with those words. All she could do was smile and raise her glass to her sister.

"Congratulations!"

For several minutes, almost a quarter of an hour, they both were silent, lost in their own thoughts about the momentousness of this moment. Finley finally broke the silence.

"I refuse to wear pink."

By the time they walked up the hill to the hotel, they were convinced that they had walked off all the calories associated with finishing off a bottle of champagne and three tiers of sandwiches, cakes, and scones, complete with clotted cream and jam. Whitt came into the lobby giggling and leaning on Finley's arm. They recovered some modicum of decorum by the time they reached the desk.

"Miss Blake, we have put your guest in his room."

Whitt's face straightened. "What time is it?"

"5:30 p.m., ma'am."

Whitt looked at Finley and started toward the room. "I guess he got in early."

"I'll just say hello and then leave you two alone."

"No need to rush off. He'll be here for a couple of days."

"I know, but..."

David stood in the door. If he had any doubt about whether Whitt cared for him, the flood of tears she shed answered everything.

Whitt never cries. God, what she was holding inside! Poor kid. She loves him. I hope he loves her enough to agree to her conditions, however silly, just so they can be together.

"How's it going?" David looked at Finley, as he wiped at Whitt's tears with his handkerchief. She was sitting on his lap in the ante room of his suite. How she got there, Whitt couldn't remember.

"Good. Did you have a pleasant trip?" Finley responded, smiling softly at the dazed look on her sister's face.

"Yeah, uneventful. Which is the best kind." David was still dabbing at Whitt's eyes. She had settled her head against his shoulder, but the tears wouldn't stop.

"Ain't that the truth. Look, I'll let you take care of her. She can come get her stuff later."

Finley softly closed the door to their room and headed across the courtyard to hers. She put the key in the door and sighed heavily. Her heart contracted and released, only to seize again. *I'm happy for her. But I am jealous. I miss Max. I miss him so much.*

Try as she might to stem them, the tears slipped out and spilled silently down her cheek. She put her satchel on the corner table and headed into the sitting room, kicking off her shoes as she went. *Guess I should get used to having dinner alone for the next couple of days.*

From the corner of her eye, she saw movement in the filtered darkness. Her body tensed reflexively.

"I hope you don't mind me taking a Coke from the mini-bar."

Finley's knees almost gave way. She covered her mouth with her hand and let herself be swallowed up in Max's embrace. Hot tears stung her face. *I must look like such a fool, but I don't really care. He's here. Max is here.*

At seven o'clock, Finley slipped a note under the door of the other room and headed over to the bar. She and Max sat in the little bar room alone, for which she was glad. She wanted him all to herself.

"What can I get you?" Max had his arm around her even as they sat. His words suggested that he was getting up, but his actions confirmed that he had her and he wasn't letting go.

She touched the laugh lines around his mouth and kissed the tiny etches around his eyes. He buried his head in the valley of her neck and rested it there, until he raised his head and found her lips. It was in this position that Whitt and David found them some minutes later.

Whitt was confused at what she saw. She couldn't readily tell who the couple was. She thought she recognized her sister's embroidered peasant blouse. And the mop of dark hair in which the woman's fingers were entwined seemed vaguely familiar. But she couldn't imagine her sister kissing any man but Max, and Max was in Delhi. She looked at David who was smiling knowingly.

"Max?" Whitt's voice was quiet, almost timid.

Finley and Max pulled apart, a bit startled.

"Whitt, David. Sorry, we didn't hear you come in. The bartender has gone to get ice," Max laughed softly under his breath. They had been caught out. Better Whitt and David than some stranger.

Whitt crossed the room and playfully punched Max's arm. "Whatever are you doing here?"

David and Max exchanged a glance.

"I was going to surprise Fin this weekend and mentioned it to David. And then you called."

Whitt looked more confused than ever. "So, you were planning this even before I called?"

David nodded. "I missed you too much. I figured the worst that could happen was you'd kick me to the curb. But at least I'd know."

Whitt touched David's cheek, and the tears started again. "I'd never do that."

When the bartender returned with a bucket of ice, the group ordered their drinks. Champagne for the Blake sisters, a Lion beer for David, and whiskey neat for Max. They didn't really need ice, but no one had the heart to tell the young man who covered the bar.

"The Four Musketeers, back together again!" Max said jokingly, looking at David. "Let's hope we can keep them out of trouble this time, better than we did last time."

When they were last all together in Morocco, Whitt and Finley had been kidnapped, almost snake-bitten, and nearly shot. David and Max had wondered how two seemingly normal young women could find so much trouble in such a short time.

"You make it sound like we go looking for it," Whitt retorted. "It finds us!"

"Well, let's just play it low-key and hope that the strange goings-on continue to have nothing to do with us," Finley said.

"What 'strange goings-on'?" David had shifted his position on one of the banquettes so that he had a clear view of both Whitt, who sat snuggled beside him, and Finley across the small room.

"Do you want to tell them or shall I?" Finley replied.

David and Max sat open-mouthed as Whitt recounted the events of the past two weeks. Samantha's death was the most startling occurrence since Max's departure and Whitt's arrival, but the simian rampage and the elephant charge had also left both women feeling a little apprehensive. They hadn't realized until Whitt began to relay the series of events what danger they had been in.

"But you find us happy and whole!" Finley felt the need to add some element of assurance, if only to comfort herself in the face of the outrageous saga that Whitt had just shared. As much as she tried, she still felt discomforted by the events that seemed random, but still left her with a niggling sense that they were, unfortunately, somehow connected.

David spoke first, breaking the silence that had fallen on the room. The only sound, until his voice had cracked through the wall of unspoken fear that invaded the room, was the squeak as the bartender wiped dry the glasses he had just cleaned. The foursome had watched, wordless after Whitt's account, as the young man inspected each glass, holding it to the light to check for water spots.

"What's the plan for tomorrow?" David asked, in his nonchalant California way, wholly comfortable with the non sequitur.

Finley picked up on his cue to change the subject, "I think we're heading to Yala for the day. Whitt?"

By the time Whitt had laid out the itinerary for the day, another round of drinks had been consumed and David, ever hungry, was thinking about food.

"Are we eating here or heading somewhere else?"

"Why don't we try dinner here since it's getting late and we have an early morning?" Max suggested.

Accordingly, they headed to the dining room for a sumptuous Sri Lankan meal, accompanied by boisterous laughter and embellished stories that filled in the past several months of their lives since they had last been together. It was well after midnight before they staggered back to their rooms.

"Let me get my stuff so I don't have to bother you guys in the morning," Whitt said, looking at her watch with a frown. "Or rather in a few hours."

She headed to the closet and reached for her duffel and backpack, opening the pack as she turned toward the bed.

"What is this?" She pulled out a shiny metal square. "Richard's key ring! How did it get in here?"

She held in her hand the key ring thumb drive that had attracted both Finley's and a wanton monkey's attention in the past week.

"Strange. I can't imagine how it got into my backpack." Whitt mused.

"Whatever. Just leave it there, and we'll deal with it later. It's too late to try to figure it out now," Finley said sleepily as Whitt dropped the key ring on the desk and headed out.

"Gladly. As long as it doesn't summon flying monkeys," Whitt said as she headed to her room.

MORNING CAME TOO SOON. THE driver and guide that were to take them to Yala arrived at 4:30 a.m. Whitt had added David and Max's name to the tour list the night before, but it didn't really matter since they had rented a private car for the trip.

The guide endeared himself to Finley and Whitt by offering them a mug of strong coffee laced with condensed milk. While Finley normally took her coffee black, she knew that the shot of glucose would keep her running at least until they were on the road to Yala. Shortly after Koggala, where they saw the stilt fishermen, Max had leaned his head back for a nap with Finley stretched out near him, her head in his lap. In the seat behind, David and Whitt had curled up, his arm around her, her head on his shoulder.

When they arrived at Yala some two and a half hours later, the sun was up, and the damp chill was gone. The guide explained that in Sri Lanka, "the big five" was made up of leopards, elephants, sloth bears, sperm whales, and blue whales. The group would only be seeing three of the five today, in addition to indigenous deer, monkeys, crocodiles, and myriad birds.

Yala, as Finley had rightly remembered, was a photographer's paradise. She had brought extra cameras, and a bag full of other equipment. Max had been gracious enough to carry the extra satchel, so that she didn't have to make choices about which lenses, filters, and tripods to bring. He liked to see her work, watching her brow furrow and her eyes narrow with concentration as she zeroed in on a subject.

They were in the park no more than three minutes when the camera shutter started clicking. Finley had spotted a leafless tree on a small mound in one of the watering holes that had reflected its image back into the water. The shot she composed was of upper and lower pools of blue, cut by a sliver of dark earth, into which the tree and its reflection, like hands, reached into the sky above and the water below. Stark, spare, and breathtaking.

As they moved deeper into the park, the wildlife seemed to come alive. Elephants lifted their trunks through the brush to get a better grasp on upper leaves, several with calves by their sides or under their legs. Groups of water buffalo and sambar, a deer indigenous to Sri Lanka, were scattered about the flats, sharing space in the wetlands with crocodiles of monstrous size.

"If I were that deer, I would take a step back," Whitt said, observing a group of spotted deer inching dangerously close to what looked like a submerged log, but in reality was a large croc.

Near Elephant Rock, the guide pointed out a cluster of trees that were covered with langurs, a type of white-bearded leaf monkey. They were perched precariously on branches, even at the topmost parts of the trees.

"How do they do that?" Max had seized a pair of binoculars and was trying to figure out how monkeys of that size could balance themselves on the spidery upper branches of the barren, seemingly dead trees.

"The trees may look brittle, but they are quite strong, even in the dry season," the guide explained. "These monkeys have lived in this region for centuries and have evolved to suit the environment."

Just then, a crackle came across the radio. Kasun, the guide, turned in his seat, even as he reached to grab the handhold above his head.

"Hold on. Leopards!"

The jeep kicked up funnels of dust behind it as it struck out across the dry roadbed. They were apparently headed toward a large tree that stood alone in the middle of a dry field that looked like just the right kind of tender for a wildfire. They weren't alone in their rush to see the leopards, either. Like tumbleweeds, other swirls of dust, signaling more arriving jeeps, made a beeline for the tree.

A large male sprawled out on one of the branches, turning his head from time to time so that the amateur photographers below could catch his best angles. Finley watched his spots catch the light through her telephoto lens. Had he not moved, he could easily have blended into the dappled sunlight without anyone but a trained eye knowing he was there. *I wonder how many villagers were ambushed in just such a scene in the days before the preserve was established. Messy.*

Something made Finley shift her lens angle just slightly. There, in the viewfinder, she caught sight of members of the "German" tour group that she had seen in Nuwara Eliya. Among them was Lena van Dijk. Finley scanned the group looking for her dashingly handsome husband. *You are going straight to hell, girl. Scoping for that woman's husband. And while your guy is sitting right beside you. Shame. And you talked about Whitt!*

"Anyone want to use the telephoto lens to see the leopard? You can get a really clear view of him." Finley held the camera out. David reached for it.

"If you don't mind," he grinned. "And I promise not to break it."

"Can you get a good view with the binoculars?" Finley had moved closer to Max, lining up his angle to see what he might be looking at from this vantage point.

"Yeah. These are great!" Max took the binoculars away from his eyes and held them toward her. She shook her head at the offer, and he turned back to take another look at the leopard that had been joined in the tree by a smaller cat, presumably a female. "This is phenomenal! Two of them!"

Finley smiled at his enthusiasm. It made her wonder what he had been like as a boy. She picked up another one of her cameras and fitted it with an ultra-wide-angle lens. The leopards were still visible, but the wider landscape came into focus with a kind of fish-eye perspective.

She had never used this one before—another suggestion of her go-to guy at 47th Street Photo back in Manhattan. Satisfied with the shots of the leopards she had gotten with the telephoto lens, she was ready to experiment with her new gadget.

She focused initially on the tree, specifically the leopards so that they were sharp against the landscape. After a few test shots, she began to play with what was in focus and what was peripheral. She switched on the auto-shutter as she panned the camera slowly to the left and then to the right, trying to keep the lens level with the horizon. She now understood why the tech at the camera shop had tried to convince her to buy the panoramic head for her tripod. Next time.

"Are you catching anything prizeworthy?" Whitt had taken her binoculars from her eyes and was looking at her sister play with the new lens. She turned to Max. "You should see some of the shots she has gotten. If she doesn't enter them in something, I will!"

Finley blushed at her sister's praise. "I'm still learning, but I'm having fun."

Max saw Finley's embarrassment and smiled. "You'll have to show them to me when we get back to the hotel. You've turned into a regular paparazzo and forgot to tell me."

At Kasun's suggestion, Gayan, their driver, reversed the jeep and separated from the crowd that was growing around the treed leopards.

"This park has the highest concentration of leopards in the world, so we are likely to see others as we drive around," Kasun remarked. "And a sighting of a sloth bear is even rarer than seeing a leopard. They are camera-shy!"

As the day progressed, herds of elephants crossed their paths and even ambled alongside them at one point, affording Finley an up-close-and-personal shot of a young calf trying to catch up to its mother after having seemingly gotten distracted. *A far cry from the charge we experienced in Udawalawe.* Water buffalo, sambar, and spotted deer populated the scenery at every turn. David had passed the larger camera back to Finley and returned to watching the flora and fauna through binoculars.

Twice on the trek along the nearly empty trails, Kasun, who had proved to be a skilled tracker, quietly pointed into the bush. In the first instance, a young leopard sat perched on a rock behind the cover of tall grasses and thorny scrub brush. Finley had been able to catch a shot of the creature, its eyes following the jeep, its body unmoving. When she turned to catch a last glance, the cat was gone.

When Gayan slowed the jeep a second time, it was to catch fleeting glimpses of a female with a young cub moving between the grasses like shadows. Finley switched the shutter to silent and auto, turning the telephoto lens in that general direction, hoping she might capture something worth saving, besides the memory.

As the sun dipped behind the trees, the driver headed the jeep toward the exit. Puffs of dust could be seen on the horizon as guides made last-ditch efforts to allow their passengers a quick sighting of a leopard before the park closed.

"No sloth be…" Whitt had just started to lament the absence of sloth bears this trip to Yala, when Gayan pulled over to let one lumber down the middle of the road. Finley snapped a portrait with the telephoto lens before pulling out the fish-eye to capture the bear and its "long walk home."

"Now it's complete!" Finley said with finality. She had seen her big three, but the greater pleasure had been seeing two grown men squeal with joy at the monkeys, leopards, and elephants like little boys at the circus.

She turned to Max, who was still following the track of the bear as it ambled home. "Did you have fun?"

He turned and kissed her fully in response. "Thank you!"

She settled back in his arms for her long ride home.

It was almost eight o'clock when they reached Galle and turned toward the hotel. The red and blue flashing lights caught Kasun's attention long before the jeep got fully up the hill.

"I wonder what's going on." He hopped out of the vehicle to ask one of the police officers who were gathered in front of Dutch House. The narrow street was blocked by several cars with flashing lights, as well as an ambulance.

Whitt, roused from sleeping on David's shoulder by the flashing lights, snapped awake. "Do you think Paul's OK? He is rather old."

"He isn't that old, but that doesn't mean that he couldn't have taken ill." Finley paused. "But you wouldn't have that many police for a heart attack." Finley pulled herself into a sitting position and strained to see who was in the ambulance.

"Maybe we should wait here until Kasun gets back. No point in us asking the same questions if he's got the answers," Max said.

Within minutes, Kasun returned to the car. "It appears there has been an accident. A young man has died."

"Where? There were no other guests on our side and all the people at the Gardens are older." Whitt was trying to work out who could have been the victim, given the description Kasun gave.

"Can we get to our rooms or is everything cordoned off?" Max asked.

"The police officer said we could let you off and then go back down the hill since we were not involved, but he asked that you go into the lobby area and wait before going to your rooms." Kasun looked apologetic about the inconvenience of having to wait to go to their rooms after such a long day.

"No problem," David said. He was the first out and helped Whitt and Finley collect their backpacks and satchels. He pulled out some bills for a tip and passed it to Gayan and Kasun. "Thanks for a memorable day!"

For all the activity outside, the lobby was eerily quiet. The receptionist looked visibly distressed. The foursome, following the instructions of a police officer at the door, took seats in the lobby sitting area and waited.

After a few minutes, a middle-aged man approached them. He was wearing a dark-brown suit that might have been crisper earlier in the day but was sadly wilting now. "I am Inspector Dan Pinto of the Greater Galle Police. Could you please give me your names? Are you all guests here?"

With their names written down, he proceeded with his questioning. "As your driver may have told you, there has been an accident."

"Kasun said someone had died. Who was it?"

"A young man named Oliver McNair, according to the identification that was found on his body."

Both Whitt and Finley gasped, almost simultaneously. Whitt had started to tear up. Finley's hand flew to her mouth. She was shaking her head as if that would make the tragedy less true.

"He was leaving for the Maldives tomorrow or the next day to go diving," Finley said. Max, seeing her reaction, had taken her hand, his eyes searching her face.

"You knew this man?" The inspector hovered over the two women, who were seated facing each other on matching leather couches.

"We met him in Udawalawe earlier in the week. He was in our safari group," Whitt said.

"And then we saw him in Galle Fort our first day here. He joined us for coffee."

"Was he staying at this hotel?" The inspector's eyes narrowed slightly.

"Not that we know of. You would have to ask reception," Whitt offered.

"They say he was not a guest. Perhaps he was coming to visit *you*." The inspector put emphasis on the last word. He peered down, vulture-like, as he waited for the response. "Your number was in his phone."

"We exchanged numbers when we were in Udawalawe. Finley was going to send him some pictures, but he would have had no reason to come visit us. She would've emailed them. And we never invited him here." Whitt was starting to get angry at the implied accusation. "We've been in Yala all day. Why he was here, we don't know."

"What time did you leave for Yala? Perhaps he hoped to speak with you this morning," the inspector mused.

"We left at 4:30 a.m. You can check with reception and the tour operator. I hardly think a rational person would hope to speak with us at that hour. He would've known the tours leave early," Finley responded. "And if not, when he came to speak with us, he would have found us gone, and presumably would've left after that."

The inspector, having failed to tie either Whitt or Finley to the victim besides being casual acquaintances, was visibly frustrated. "You may go to your rooms, but please do not leave the grounds until my officers have taken a full statement."

As she stood to leave, Finley turned to the inspector. "If you don't mind my asking, how did he die?"

The inspector hesitated a moment and then replied, "The cause of death is unknown at present."

"Thank you, Inspector."

The inspector surveyed them carefully as they filed from the room.

"Poor Oliver!" Whitt said. They had all gathered in Max and Finley's room to assess the situation and consider what to do next.

"He was so looking forward to his diving expedition," Finley smiled sadly, remembering his excitement.

"I wish there were something that we could do. Perhaps we can think of something over a drink," Whitt suggested. "I think we could all use one."

"Since we can't leave the grounds I think we will have to have that drink as well as dinner here again tonight," Max said.

"It's just as well. I'm too tired to move anyway," Finley said. "See you in thirty minutes?"

When the door closed, Finley turned to Max. "Something isn't right. What was he doing here? He wasn't staying here. He wasn't looking for us. Who or what was he looking for?"

She was pacing the room as she talked. "We don't even know if he was who he said he was. That's two deaths in two weeks. That's two too many!"

"You're starting to look like me with that pacing," Max said, patting the sofa beside him. "Come sit down. Calm yourself."

Finley listened to the "sit down" part and took a seat, but she found it hard to calm herself. No sooner had she sat down, she popped back up and went to the desk. The key ring was still there. She picked it up and put it in the pocket of her camera case. That hadn't been what he was looking for. She couldn't fathom why she had even thought to make that connection.

"What's this all about? These things must be related." Her voice was strained, her brow furrowed as she punched each word, stabbing the air as she spoke. "I know they are. But I don't know how."

"Why don't we get washed up and head to dinner? We can discuss it then." Max put his arms around Finley's waist and pulled her to him. "You'll figure it out."

He continued, "Whether I want you to or not." He kissed her forehead and then her lips. "Just don't get hurt!"

"I am not getting involved. I just want to figure out how the pieces fit."

"But figuring out the pieces may get you involved. And that may get you hurt. Be careful."

Over dinner, the conversation focused on what they knew and didn't know about Oliver. They had opted for drinks at the table. A few of the other guests, namely the Liebners and the couple that had been identified as Dutch from Leiden, were sitting sullenly in the little bar room. The heaviness of their silence, coupled with the closeness of the room, would have made for awkwardness at best.

"Do you know when Oliver got here?" Max asked, trying to get Whitt and Finley to share the storm of thoughts and emotions that were raging in their heads.

Whitt contemplated the question for a moment before responding. "I can't remember if he said. He said he was in Galle for a couple of days before he headed off to dive."

"I think he mentioned that he was on a two-week vacation, so that would suggest that he had spent a week somewhere else," Finley said. "I don't recall seeing him in Nuwara Eliya."

"Did he say where he was staying?" David asked. "We've established that he wasn't staying here."

"When he left us after coffee, he did say he was going to swing by his room to drop off some gifts before heading to the lighthouse." Finley remembered him heading off toward the palisades.

She knew Whitt wouldn't be able to remember. She had been so in her own little world of misery, pining for David. *Someone could have lit her foot on fire and she would've been clueless.*

"OK, you said there were two deaths. Do you think he knew the other victim?" Max was trying to help Finley connect her dots, but he was starting to think she was grasping at straws.

"I don't think so. As I said, I don't remember seeing him in Nuwara Eliya."

"Then let's go through who you do remember seeing in which places, and then see if there is any pattern." Max was successful as a consultant for this very reason. He approached problems methodically. All problems except those of the heart. Those he tended to drown in drink. Luckily, Finley had thrown him a lifeline just in time when they were in Morocco last year.

David pulled a pen and small spiral notebook from his coat pocket. "OK, shoot. Start at Nuwara Eliya since that is where the first person died. Unless things were wonky before that."

"No, I think Nuwara Eliya was the start," Whitt said as she and Finley listed the people they had seen in multiple locations.

"Wait, we have to go back to Kandy at least. Maybe even further back," Finley interrupted, turning to Whitt. "Remember? We have seen folks from a couple of tour groups in several places. Polonnaruwa, Helga's, all over Nuwara Eliya."

"This is getting too complicated," Whitt grumbled, playing with a forkful of food. "It's giving me a headache. And I'm not sure it's going to make a difference."

"You may be right. The police may think we are suspects," Finley added. "And we don't have anyone like Evans to make sense of the loose ends." Max smiled at the mention of Evans. Inspector Gareth Evans. Senior officer at Interpol. And a rival, however much Finley might say otherwise, for his girl's affection.

12

"**A**FTERNOON TEA IS SUCH A civilized activity," Max said, reaching for another smoked-salmon finger sandwich. He and Whitt had devoured the first batch so quickly that the waiter had brought another large plate stacked high with a mix of sandwiches, heavy on the smoked salmon. David just shook his head. The scones were his favorite, while Finley had gone for the strawberry tarts.

They were sitting in the Galle Fort Hotel. The inspector had allowed them to leave the grounds, having secured their rather pithy statement. "We know nothing of the death of Oliver McNair. We were in Yala before, during, and after his death."

From what the housekeepers had said, it appeared that Oliver hadn't been stabbed or strangled. He had been found sprawled out in the center courtyard, not far from the pool. There was no blood near his body. The maids were speculating that it was black magic, although one said that poison was more likely.

The housekeeper said that her mother had read of another death of a foreign national in Nuwara Eliya that had baffled the police.

Her mother had said it was black magic. "Just because it didn't happen in the south, doesn't mean that the sorcerer didn't cast his spell."

"I cannot believe that the only connection we have between the two deaths is black magic," Finley said half-laughingly as she recalled the conversation she had overheard outside her door. She suspected that the maids had wanted her to hear for whatever reason, and had spoken in halting English rather than Sinhala, the common language among locals.

"It doesn't really matter how they died, only that the method seems to be similar," Whitt added. "The question still is who knew them both and wanted them dead."

"Why is it that every time we sit down to eat with you two, death comes up as a topic?" David was smiling at Whitt as he raised the question, knowing that he was going to get a playful punch for his irreverence. He intercepted the punch by kissing Whitt's hand. The acerbic retort she had planned withered. She shook her head at his ability to disarm her so easily.

"Well, at least we have something pleasant to look forward to," Whitt said. "Paul was quite generous inviting us all to sit with him in the box at elephant polo tomorrow."

Paul had extended his earlier invitation to the Sunday elephant polo match to Max and David, asking them to join him in the owners' box. That meant that Whitt and Finley spent the morning scouring Galle to find hats appropriate for the occasion.

Having found a shop in Galle that stocked fascinators and other high-end fashion, Whitt had decided to add another dress to her wardrobe—this time a navy, pin-tucked, grass-linen, belted maxi. Finley had followed suit with a flowy, flowered thing that she knew she would probably never wear again, but had bought because she liked the feel of the lightweight silk against her skin. Instead of ostrich-plumed fascinators, they both had gone with practical, large straw hats—Whitt's in matching navy and Finley's natural with a black grosgrain band.

"How far do we have to go? I can't image that there is a place for elephants to play near the city," Finley asked.

"Paul said that the Gymkhana Club grounds were actually just outside the fort. So, not far at all," Max replied.

"Where do they keep the elephants, then? Are there stables for elephants like there are for horses?" Whitt asked.

"I guess we'll find out tomorrow."

The polo grounds looked like any big football or soccer field, except that people milled around with champagne in hand instead of beer, most in flouncy dresses and fancy headgear instead of team shirts. A section of the green had been closed off for the elephants, the mahouts, and the riders. Riders and their trainers were taking the elephants through their paces, making sure that there was enough room between animals to prevent them from getting spooked, that riders knew how to mount and dismount properly, and that the animals were watered before the match began.

The sport had supposedly begun in Sri Lanka during the British colonial era but was claimed by Nepal as having been its invention in 1982. In Sri Lanka, play was suspended for almost fifteen years in response to animal activists' protests. But three years ago, Gymkhana Club reintroduced the match as an annual fundraising event after addressing the concerns raised.

When the foursome arrived in a car hired by Paul, they were escorted around the risers to a section under cover from the sun, which was getting oppressively hot.

"I'm so glad we are wearing something that breathes," Whitt said, turning to Max. "Aren't you hot in that blazer?"

Both Max and David had opted for lightweight linen blazers. Max was in a classic-navy double-breasted, and David was in a tweedy wheat slouch, the sleeves of which he had already pushed up to reveal muscular, tanned forearms.

"It's not too bad. About the same as Morocco or India." Max had opted to put his jacket over a navy polo shirt and straw-colored linen pants. His favorite play of blue on blue had brightened the teal in his eyes. Working under the sun in India had bronzed his skin and deepened the creases of his laugh lines. Finley sighed softly at the sight of him.

She took Max's arm as they ascended the stairs to their box. *These boys are easy on the eye, and the ladies here seem to know how to appraise new horseflesh when they see it.* Several women had stopped their conversations to nod as the group made their way around the aisle. Paul rose to greet them as they approached his box.

"So glad that you are here! Let me introduce you around." Paul turned to two other couples in the box. One woman was a banker and her husband was headmaster at one of the private schools in Colombo. The other couple were local restaurateurs, with places in Colombo and Galle.

"Tom and I own Taprobane a few miles away from here with another partner. Sherri runs the place in Colombo. You should all come out to the island. If that police inspector ever finishes with us," Paul said wearily.

He was trying desperately to keep his guests occupied since the police had asked that all guests at Dutch House stay in the vicinity. The inspector had reluctantly agreed to let Max and David catch their scheduled flights out the next morning after verifying their particulars.

"The guys will be heading out tomorrow, but maybe Finley and I will take you up on your offer," Whitt said. "We have a few things to do tomorrow. We're doing a cooking course! But maybe later in the week for lunch."

David leaned over to Whitt when they finally sat down to champagne and canapés.

"Those 'few things' wouldn't happen to include buying a few more baubles, would it?" He smiled, turning his attention to the match that was about to begin.

"And if it does?" Whitt kissed him on the cheek and shrugged. "You know I've been a crow since before you met me. I like shiny things!"

"And I love you for it!" David returned her kiss with one of his own, but his claimed her lips. "Get yourself something shiny from me, and we'll settle it when you get home."

"How kind of you!" Whitt smiled. She knew just which new stone she was going to add to her collection. Their cooking class didn't start until just before lunch, so they would have plenty of time to run past the jeweler and commission something else.

Finley saw the wheels in her sister's head turning. She smiled at David and shook her head. *If there is something more to be bought, Whitt will find it. That poor boy better make a lot of money with that Moldovan wine. Whitt's going to spend her money and his too!*

Whitt was surprised at how fast elephants could run. She shouldn't have been, after experiencing the elephant charge. The matches were set up the same as polo on ponies. There were chukkas like in polo, and the object of the game was the same—to hit the ball with the mallet so that it went into the goal. The only thing different was the animal used to play the game, which were elephants instead of horses—or ponies, as one gentleman was quick to point out.

Unlike polo on horseback, though, each of the elephants had two riders: a mahout, or handler, who sat just behind the elephant's ears, and a player who sat behind the mahout using a long mallet to strike the ball. Often the players would grab their mahout around the waist for leverage as they swung down to get closer to the ball. This year, the local Sri Lankan teams were playing against each other for a 500,000-rupee prize. The tournament, however, was more about pride and bragging rights than money.

Finley had brought a smaller camera that she could easily fit into her satchel. She had somehow managed to find a way to get the telephoto lens to conform to the contours of her bag so that it wasn't too obvious. Shortly after sitting down, she had grabbed a few shots that captured the energy of the crowd. She was dying to go into the cordoned areas and take pictures of the elephants, but she didn't dare ask. Instead, she satisfied herself with shots of the people, their hats, and the mahouts that wandered by.

Once the matches started, she took a few quick shots and then put her camera away.

"What, you aren't going to shoot the action?" Max said as she zipped her satchel and sat back.

"Nope. I'm not working today. I'm going to enjoy the polo, the people, and the champagne without a camera in my hand."

"Oh, dear. That means I have to keep up my end of the conversation," Max teased.

"Have I been neglecting you with this damn camera?" Finley asked, suddenly serious. "I'm so sorry. I get carried away. I'm so glad that you are here!"

Max tucked her arm in his and winked at her. "You've looked after me very well. I cannot complain."

The next two hours were filled with lumbering elephants, agile players, and skilled mahouts until, at last, there was a winner. Victory went to the team from Ella, who had missed a win the previous year by one goal. Feeling vindicated, they sprayed each other and their mounts with champagne.

"What a waste of good bubbly!" Whitt was incensed by the antics. "I have never understood that practice."

Paul and the others had gone down to the field to congratulate the winners and engage in the picture taking. Paul, forever the promoter, rarely missed a photo op that might position him and his properties among the jet-set crowd. Finley admired him in that regard, even as she and Whitt had the sense that every conversation he had was pre-calculated to maximize his advantage.

"Do you mind if we people-watch and wait until the crowd clears a bit?" Finley asked. "It'll take a while before the car can reach us."

"No problem. I like watching the beautiful people." David was taking in the mass of people in front of him. In fact, all four of them were facing forward, scanning the crowd for the most fashionable, the most famous, and the most ostentatious.

Finley thought she saw the van Dijks among the throng on the far side of the field. The polo match, elephant or not, would seem the sort of place that Lena, with her lithe figure and ice-blond presence, and Alfred, with his classically sculpted handsomeness, would frequent. When she looked back, they were gone. Another perfect, beautiful couple had taken their place.

"Since we are off the hill, shall we stay down for dinner?" David was hungry again. *How that boy can eat that much and still maintain that six-pack is beyond me. What Whitt eats up in jewelry, David consumes in food.*

"Fine with me. Ladies?" Max looked at the two sisters for agreement, and they nodded in response.

As expected, both Amangalla and Aqua Fort had lines out the door. Many from the polo crowd had stayed at the Club for dinner, while the rest had headed into town. Paul had invited Finley, Whitt, and the crew to join them, but no one felt like socializing with strangers. It was their last night together, and they wanted to make it special. Just the Four Musketeers.

Surprisingly, Fort Printers had a table for four outside near the pool. The restaurant used to be a mansion where the Fort Printer Company had run an old printing press using wood-block lettering and wrought-iron presses. The presses were shuttered in 2002, and the building was turned into a boutique hotel and restaurant. When the champagne came, Max raised his glass. "To lasting friendship and everlasting love!"

The group nodded in agreement. What more was there to say.

The goodbyes the next morning were long and bittersweet. The seven o'clock departure time didn't help make them any easier. They had ordered coffee on the veranda and both Whitt and Finley came to breakfast in their pajamas.

"Don't you look sweet," David said laughingly. He was looking at the *My Little Pony* T-shirt Finley was wearing with her sweatpants.

Finley chuckled, "You can never accuse a Blake sister of seducing a man." She glanced at her sister's rumpled, oversized cotton pajamas.

"When do you get back?" David had pulled Whitt onto his lap as he finished his coffee.

"In ten days. And, as much as I love my sister, I will be counting every day," Whitt said. "I miss you already."

Finley and Max grabbed their coffee and stepped back into their room to give Whitt and David—and themselves—a bit more privacy.

"You coming to me? Or do you have another assignment lined up?" Max had sidled up behind Finley and put his arms around her waist as she stood at the door that opened to the pool.

They had talked about her coming to Delhi to work on an extended project that would keep them together for at least a while. But Max knew that she was a journalist at heart, and that if a compelling assignment came up, she would probably take it.

"To you."

Max registered his approval by turning her around and kissing her firmly. Her heart ached. She knew it would only be a few days before they were together again, but even those few days seemed too long.

"You'll call me when you get in?" she finally said, touching his cheek and then tracing his laugh lines with her finger.

"Then and every day after until you get home."

13

NEITHER SISTER FELT LIKE GOING back to sleep after Max and David left. They were more restless than sleepy. Besides, Whitt had to move her things back into her old room within the next few hours, and she knew that if she fell asleep, she would be out for most of the day.

"Let's get dressed and wander. The appointment with the jeweler isn't until ten o'clock and the class starts at eleven-thirty, so we have three hours of unstructured time," Whitt said. "Whatever will we do with it!"

"Well, I know one thing—we're going to find more coffee!"

They ended up at Heritage Café, which followed tourist-waking hours, opening at eight-thirty instead of the more common ten o'clock start. They sat with big mugs of coffee and talked about the shops they had wandered past along Pedlar Street on their way down the hill.

Located in a historic building from the 1600s, the café was quickly becoming a hangout for artists, writers, and creatives of Sri Lanka. The artwork that decorated the café—sculptures and wallscapes made from reclaimed material in bright colors and varied textures—signaled the vibe. A few of the patrons toward the back of the room, presumably artists who had spent the night painting instead of sleeping, hung over their cups, their scraggy hair masking their paint-marked faces.

Across the courtyard, sitting over coffee and breakfast, Whitt recognized the Campbells, the young newlywed couple that the sisters had met in Kandy. They mouthed a hello and went back to their conversation and food.

"Such a cute couple," Whitt said, smiling wistfully at the Campbells' apparent joy at being in each other's company.

"That'll be you soon," Finley laughed as those words prompted her sister to almost choke on her next bite of curd and treacle. She patted her on the back and changed the subject. "What new hunk of stone are you going after this time?"

"I will never be that starry-eyed," Whitt said under her breath, rolling her eyes. She picked up on the jewelry cue and continued, "I think I know what stone I want and how I want it done. David and I talked about it, but I know I'm going to change my mind, so I'm afraid to say. Are you getting anything?"

"No, I need more jewelry like I need a hole in my head."

Despite that, Finley walked out of the jewelers with a pair of moonstone earrings to match her strands, muttering to herself about not needing any more jewelry that she wasn't going to wear. Whitt had spent the better part of an hour working with the designers to fit a large, green raw tourmaline with blue undertones into a silver bezel setting.

To keep her sister occupied, Whitt had sent one of the salespeople after Finley, showing her trays of already-set stones in creative, modern designs. Finley had made the mistake of pausing over a pair of earrings, and Whitt had picked up on the hesitation. Next thing Finley knew, the earrings were wrapped and put in her hand. Her protests went unheard.

"You will be so glad you got them," Whitt said. "Besides, Mama and Daddy said to get you something for your birthday and these will be perfect."

By the time they had reached the cooking class, Finley had quieted down, silently pleased with her new acquisition. The class, held in the kitchen of Jag Bevan, was taught by the founder of the Tasting Spoon. The chef may have left the restaurant's kitchen, but he never abandoned his love of cooking. There were only five students in the class: Finley, Whitt, a woman of Sri Lankan heritage named Prisha, who lived in London but had come back to find her roots, and of all people, the Lockes.

"We seem to be following the same itinerary," Helen said, embracing the sisters. "Our German friends are ending their tour, and so are we. But we had an extra day after they left and nothing to do, so the concierge at the hotel nicely found this for us. It should be fun."

Richard looked less than enthused, but he proved to be quite handy in the kitchen once the class started. The instructor had them make shrimp with curry leaves and green beans, which was served with stir-fried noodles instead of rice, and *watalappam*, a jaggery-based, spice-laced pudding, for dessert.

Finley could have skipped the shrimp main dish, which if paired with any other dessert, would have had her attention and praise. Her focus this time, however, was on the dessert.

The cardamom-flavored coconut flan had been one of her favorite sweets since her first trip to the island. While she appreciated the intricacy of flavors that comprised the shrimp curry, she lost herself in the combinations of textures that made up the flan. She closed her eyes to savor the smooth richness of the custard on her tongue.

"Like that, do you?" Whitt said.

Finley opened her eyes to see the instructor, her sister, Prisha, and the Lockes staring at her as she rolled the flan about in her mouth. "Was I making sounds?" Finley asked sheepishly.

"No, but I think we got the gist of what you were thinking," Whitt teased.

Finley blushed at her sister's comment. "It's just so damn good." Richard helped her out by adding his praise to the silkiness that the coconut milk contributed to the dessert.

As they were leaving, Finley caught up to Richard. "Thank you for saving me from mortification back there. It was just so good. I couldn't help myself."

"I fully understand," Richard said. "I'm a sweets person, too. Helen likes the savories. My son took after me."

He paused, standing in the doorway that led to the street, his face registering a profound sadness. He seemed to be waiting for Helen, but Finley saw that he really had paused to recover himself after his mention of his son. She wanted to turn away to give him his privacy. Instead, she changed the subject.

"Oh, by the way, do you still have your key ring?" She waited for his response before continuing. She fully expected him to say that he had lost it.

"Yes, I have it right here. Why do you ask?"

Finley thought quickly. "I saw one that looked similar to it in one of the shops and wondered whether it was like yours. What does it have besides the key clasp?"

Richard pulled his out and showed her the flashlight and thumb drive features of the key ring before putting it back into his front pant pocket.

"It's a pretty handy little gadget," Finley remarked casually.

By the time Helen joined them with Whitt, they had moved on to talking about food, specifically the consistency of egg hoppers and other fermented breads like *injera* that they had eaten in their travels. Richard had had a hard time getting used to hoppers, but now as they were getting ready to leave, he found that he had developed a taste for them.

"Are you still talking about food after all that we have eaten?" Helen asked. "I need some tea and a nice long nap."

"When do you head home?" Whitt asked.

"Tomorrow to Colombo, and then back to England," Helen responded.

"Well, have a safe trip home," Finley said as the Lockes headed off to their hotel. "It was a pleasure meeting you."

The heavy lunch, and intense preparation that preceded it, had made Finley and Whitt less inclined to get on a bus and drive some forty minutes outside the city to the moonstone mines and the turtle sanctuary that they were slated to see that afternoon.

"Let's see if we can change our reservation for another time or another tour." Whitt was walking toward a tour kiosk that was set up at one of the intersections in the center of Galle Fort.

As she turned to head toward the tour center, Finley thought she saw Prisha peering around the corner of a building adjacent to the Lockes' hotel. *Too much sugar. I'm imagining things again. Why ever would Prisha be following the Lockes? Or us?*

The tour operator was more than understanding. "We've had someone cancel for a local walking tour of the city. Would you be interested in that instead? I will refund you the remainder of the fee."

The walking tour seemed just what the sisters needed. A guided amble around the heart of Galle Fort with a local historian who would fill them in on the rich history of the UNESCO World Heritage site. More importantly, it was a chance to walk off some of the lunch. After making the necessary adjustments in the paperwork, Finley and Whitt were introduced to their guide.

"Hello, I'm Nethmi. I will be your guide today. I am excited to show you all the beauty and history of Galle." A pretty woman with a broad smile, warm almond-colored eyes, and a heavy plait of dark hair approached Finley and Whitt.

"Hi, I'm Whitt and this is my sister, Finley. Are you from Galle Fort?"

"Yes. My family has lived in the Fort for many centuries. In fact, four generations of my family have lived in the same colonial house,"

Nethmi stated. "I like to share our history with visitors. Shall we go?" She nodded to the tour operator and led them to the street.

The tour took them through the narrow, cobbled streets of the old city—streets that had been constructed by the Portuguese, improved by the Dutch, and renovated by the British over the many centuries that Nethmi's ancestors had lived in the city. As they walked, Nethmi shared not only the history of the city and her family in it, but her own story.

She had studied history in Colombo as a scholarship student who had performed well and was rising in her career. That is, until the tsunami hit and washed her father and brothers away while they had been outside the unexpected safety of the Fort's walls. She had finished her education the summer before and started a new job in the capital only seven months prior to that. With the death of her father and brothers, she left her desk job in Colombo and returned home to look after her mother and sister.

"I am glad my father saw me graduate," she said sadly. "I started working with Dev doing these tours many years ago. This work suits me well. I actually get to use my history degree more than I did when I worked in the city."

As they wandered, Nethmi pointed out the homes of famous people—sports figures, actors, musicians, writers, millionaires, artists, and the like—who had chosen Galle as their home. Many of the names Finley and Whitt were not acquainted with. Cricketers and celebrities, known to millions of adoring fans, were just names to the sisters, who realized how limited their worldview really was.

"Let's head to the fortification and the lighthouse. When the wall was first built by the Portuguese, it was made of only earth and mud. But the Dutch added more bastions and used granite and coral to make it stronger." Nethmi pointed out a few places in the wall where pieces of coral could still be seen.

The rampart along the fort wall was crowded with school-girls in white uniforms and long pigtails tied with blue ribbons. They walked the high embankment in clumps, from which giggles periodically erupted. Lovers strolled the path or sat together in the little alcoves that punctuated the stone walls of the bastions.

Below, the sea licked the stone fortification, lapping quietly along the beach in some places and crashing against the rocks in others. Children, with their parents in tow, descended the steep stairs to get to the pebbly beach, tossing their jellies behind them as they went, eager for the cooling wet of the water in the still-hot afternoon.

Because they were early for the sunset, Nethmi, Finley, and Whitt had started from the lighthouse. It was a magnificent, white-washed obelisk that had been built in 1848 by the British. The trio slowly walked the paths heading west into the sun. The sky had been cleared of clouds and promised a spectacular sunset. Workers on the many housing renovations—which were gentrifying the older parts of the city—had started to pack up and climb down from the rickety scaffolding that laced the outside of the old buildings.

"This is Flag Rock Bastion. It is known for the crazy people who jump off into the sea below," Nethmi said as they entered a large stone circle built into the rock.

When they got to the outer edge of the bastion, Nethmi encouraged them to look down. Unlike most sections of the fortification, which were totally man-made, this section of the wall had been nestled into a natural rock formation. Many sections of the rock jutted out into the sea, but in several places, the supporting stone had been worn away so that the only thing below the wall was the water. It was here that the foolhardy took the plunge.

"Are there particular times of the year or day that they jump?" Finley asked.

"Around sunset, for whatever reason," Nethmi responded. "Some may be jumping tonight."

They continued their walk around the embankment, heading toward Triton Bastion, a station that pointed almost due west into the sun. When they reached the bastion, they parked themselves on one of the last benches left in the circle enclosure that once had been a high tower.

Sunset at Triton was a favorite pastime of locals and tourists alike. They were lucky to have found a place to station themselves. The threesome sat in reverent silence, watching the sun dip into the sea as the crowds of schoolchildren, tourists, and lovers hummed around them.

At first, they thought the screams were of Flag Rockers diving into the sea. However, they soon realized that the sound—an initial, high-pitched scream followed a cacophony of mournful wails that seemed programmed to begin at the exact moment the sun was drowned by the sea—was too close to be coming from there. It was when they saw crowds of people looking over the edge of the bastion, pointing to the nearby beach and shouting, that they realized something was wrong. Seriously wrong.

The body lying on the small beach below the high bastion walls was that of a woman. A woman they knew. It was clear from the first moment that they peered over the wall. Her hair, her clothes. Her face was obscured, but Whitt and Finley knew it was someone they had just seen. It was Prisha.

Shock hit first, then confusion, and then a deep and numb fear. As the police sirens grew nearer, the compulsion to run away grew. Finley could see it in Whitt's face. She just wanted to get away. Any place but here.

"Have you been able to understand what people are saying? What happened?" Finley asked Nethmi.

They had moved deeper into the crowd that was gathered near the entrance to the beach so that they could see what was going on. An ambulance had arrived, and the police were trying to clear a path through the throng of people so that a stretcher could get to the body on the beach.

"They are saying she was pushed, but no one saw who did it," Nethmi responded. She was talking to a woman and a man who were excitedly explaining what they knew. "He says that everyone was focused on the sunset. No one was looking around."

It would not be hard to fall into the sea or be pushed. There was no railing along the embankments. Only within the bastions. A slip—or a shove—would send one plunging into the sea or onto the beach below. It was surprising that deaths along the ramparts was not a common event.

Nethmi read Finley's mind. "One would think that more would fall into the sea, but they don't. The path is wide, so one would have to be very clumsy to fall over."

It was getting hard to see in the encroaching twilight. Even though Finley couldn't see her, Whitt's quiet said enough. She was in shock and needed to get back to the hotel.

"Do you think we can go? My sister needs to rest. I think she's pretty shaken up."

Nethmi turned and started to move Finley and Whitt away from the crowds and into a clearing.

"Do you think she can walk back to one of the hotels? We can get you a cab from there."

"I'm OK. Rattled, but I can get to a cab," Whitt answered. Her voice sounded strange, even to herself.

By the time they had found a cab, tipped Nethmi, and headed to Dutch House, night had fully settled in. Finley and Whitt made their way to their room and unlocked the door. The light from the bathroom gave them a preview of the scene they would witness even before Whitt turned on the light.

"What the hell?" Whitt flicked on the light and surveyed the wreckage. Paper was ripped and scattered all over the sitting room. The lamp on the desk was overturned, and all the books on the small table were dumped on the floor. The room looked like a war zone. In contrast, the bedroom was pristine.

"This looks like Kandy and Nuwara Eliya revisited. What the hell is going on?" Finley said angrily. "If it's monkeys again—or chimps rather—what are they looking for, and why do they keep coming to us?"

"God, I wish the guys were here," Whitt sounded weary. "I know we can take care of this, but I don't want to."

Finley was already calling the front desk. There appeared to have been a monkey break-in and housekeeping was needed, she explained. *Not to mention murders that seems to be killing off everyone we meet.*

"And can you bring two bourbons neat from the bar? Straight away!"

14

THE MORNING PAPERS CARRIED SEVERAL versions of the previous night's events. Each tried to make their report more sensational than the other. It wouldn't have taken much to make a possible murder of an innocent young woman sensational. Still, some of the papers speculated on the nature and cause of her death. One even called it a suicide.

"It says here that no one knows the identity of the young woman who died." Whitt was sipping on her second cup of coffee with butter, a trick she had learned in Mongolia several years ago and still practiced.

"How can that be? We know who she is," Finley responded. "Didn't she have any ID on her?"

"Apparently not."

"Does that mean we have to go to the police station and tell them who she is?

"I hope not. That inspector doesn't like us much," Whitt said. "Surely someone must have come forward by now."

But the reports in the afternoon journal still had the woman as an unidentified person. Whitt and Finley were in town to check on the progress of the jewelry Whitt was having made. Finley had pulled open a newspaper while she waited and read the latest news report.

As they left the jeweler, both felt adamant that they needed to say something to the police, but both were likewise determined not to go looking for trouble. Instead, they sat at the Heritage Café at an outdoor table and dialed the police.

"No, we don't know anything about her, except her name," Finley could hear Whitt explaining to whoever was on the line.

"I really don't see what us coming into the station is going to do for you. I just gave you all the information we know, which appears to be a lot more than you had before I called." Whitt was starting to get snippy. That suggested that the police officer on the line was trying to get them to come into the station to make a statement.

Finley smiled again at her sister. She was glad Whitt was handling the call. She took another sip of her coffee and stared out at the stream of people perusing the artwork and handicrafts that lined the courtyard of the café and the street beyond it.

In her mind's eye, she registered the face even before she fully focused on who it was. She tried to catch Whitt's eye, but she was deep into a rant about good Samaritans and how hassle eroded their willingness to help. By the time Whitt had hung up the phone, all that was visible was the back of the person—a baseball cap, pulled over seemingly dark hair, and a dark polo. That was all.

"We're going to have to go around to make a formal statement," Whitt sighed resignedly, dropping into a chair opposite Finley. "I told the—"

"Do you see that man with his back to us?" Finley broke in hurriedly, touching her sister's arm to get her attention.

"What man? What are you talking about?" Whitt was trying to follow Finley's line of sight to figure out what she was looking at so intently.

"That one. With the baseball cap," Finley pointed with her head in the direction of the man she was referring to. "Isn't that Evans?"

Whitt had grown silent at the mention of the Interpol inspector's name. She looked more closely at the man in the hat.

"That's not Evans! Evans is going gray, and he's taller," Whitt said. "I swear you have Evans on the brain."

She reached across and touched Finley's arm, her face registering her worry. "Is everything OK with you and Max?"

"Yes, we're fine!" Finley snapped. "That man just looked like Evans. You just saw him from the back. You didn't get a good look at him."

"If it is, then he's probably working undercover and wouldn't appreciate us blowing it," Whitt said, exasperation written large on her face. "As I was saying before you interrupted me with your latest Evans sighting, unfortunately, no good deed goes unpunished. We have to go to the station!"

Finley acknowledged her statement by calling the waiter over and paying the bill. At the station, the two were ushered into a small, windowless room and asked to wait. After several minutes, the inspector from Oliver's investigation and a woman in a uniform with a little gold braid entered the room.

"Misses Blake, my associates tell me that you have information for me." His eyes lasered in on Whitt before flicking over to Finley's face.

"Yes, as I told the person on the phone, we know the woman's name, but nothing more," Whitt started. "We were in a cooking class with her and another couple yesterday afternoon."

"So, you were acquainted with her?" Inspector Pinto asked pointedly.

"As acquainted as one gets in a two-hour class," Finley responded.

"What can you tell me about her?"

"Nothing besides her name, and that she is from overseas and came to Sri Lanka to learn more about her heritage," Whitt added.

"Where was she living?"

"London, I think," Finley answered. She watched the inspector. He was getting increasingly flustered by the alternating sources of response. One question, it was Whitt who answered, and other times, it was Finley.

"Surely you must know more than that," the inspector shot back. "Where was she born? What did she do? Who did she work for? Was she married? Did she have children?"

"We can tell you how to make *watalappam*. We were focusing on our class, not conducting an interrogation," Whitt replied. "We have interrupted our day to provide you with information that you apparently didn't have. And now you're angry with us because we don't have all the information you want."

She rose and headed for the door. "Unless you have reason to detain us, we are leaving. And if you think you do, you had better call the embassy because you are going to have an international incident on your hands. Come on, Finley."

The inspector stood and moved toward the door. "I apologize if I have not been as accommodating as I could have been, but you must understand my dilemma. I have two deaths—that of Mr. McNair and now this one—and you have knowledge of both victims."

He continued, "I don't believe in coincidence. So, can you explain this?"

Finley joined Whitt at the door. "If you are suspecting everyone who was on the embankment or in Oliver McNair's contact list, you are going to have a lot of work to do. But you can take us off the list."

She continued, "We were in Yala when Oliver died and were standing with over ten other people at least 50 meters away when the second death occurred. As we said, we were trying to help, not volunteer as suspects."

The two women did not wait for the inspector's response. He was forced to call after them when he followed them into the hall.

"Please do not leave the greater Galle area without letting us know." He stood in the door, his mouth pursed, as the sisters walked out the front door and into the street.

Whitt walked quickly to the intersection and turned left.

"Where are you going?" Finley asked, hurrying to catch up.

"Anywhere but there!" Whitt's eyes narrowed and her face flushed as she stopped to figure out where she was.

She turned to face her sister. "The nerve of that guy. To even think of us as suspects! We would have to be crazy to walk into the station and offer evidence if we had anything to do with either death."

"He is in a bad spot. We bring him information out of the blue on one murder after he has talked to us about another."

"Yeah, and if we were involved in either, the smart thing would have been to hightail it out of the country as quietly as possible."

"True, but we were already told to stay put, so we would have been in trouble if we had left anyway."

"Well, you're sure as heck going to be in trouble if you kill a second person while you're waiting to be released to travel after killing the first one. And if you did do both deeds, you don't really care what the police say."

Finley realized it was pointless to argue. And Whitt did have a good point. She also knew that however logical that argument, the inspector wasn't going to give up on the only suspects he had and would likely put a tail on them.

Sure enough, a casually dressed young man who had paused on the opposite corner, looked up from his map as soon as Finley and Whitt started up the street toward Galle Fort.

"Don't look now, but we're being followed," Finley said. "That was fast. Maybe he was going to put a tail on us anyway, and we just made it easier for him."

"I need a drink," Whitt said, heading into the hotel lobby. "If he wants one too, he can come on in. If not, he can wait outside until I drink my fill."

They ordered a bottle of Pol Roger and settled in for a long evening. The plainclothes policeman following them waited on the far side of the street.

"Shall we just have dinner here?" Finley asked once they were seated in the bar area. "We can finish our champs and head into the dining room. It's easier than having to decide where else to go. We need to take it easy tonight."

She was thinking of Whitt's sanity more than hers.

"Maybe we can get them to bring dinner here, so we don't even have to move," Whitt had closed her eyes as she took a sip of her champagne. Her forehead was scrunched up beyond belief as frustration—and maybe a bit of worry—disturbed her normally controlled countenance.

Finley signaled the waiter and asked for a menu. When they had decided their dinner, Finley returned to the subject of the two deaths.

"So, we are saying that both of these deaths are murders?" she said.

"Do you think otherwise?

"No, just confirming," Finley answered. "Do you recall seeing anyone that we even vaguely recognized when we were on the wall?"

"I was too busy watching the sunset. Which was the whole purpose for being up there in the first place."

Finley was silent. She tried to scan the mental crowd that she had gathered in her mind. The light had been waning as the sun set. There was enough light to see the body, but Finley realized that she had identified Prisha largely from her clothes and hair. What if it wasn't her?

"Could we have made a mistake?"

"About what?" Whitt asked, her eyes fixed on her sister.

"About the body."

"Even if we did, the police didn't. There was a dead woman on the beach."

"Yes, but what if it wasn't Prisha?"

"We saw her. She was dead."

"We saw a woman in clothes that looked like what Prisha had on, but we didn't see her face."

"You want to go back and ask to see the body?" Whitt was now staring incredulously at Finley.

"I'm just saying. We made an identification based on what we knew, not what we actually saw."

"Ok, let's assume it wasn't Prisha, but some other woman who died. What then? What does it matter?"

"Could someone have wanted us—or anyone, for that matter— to think that she was dead?" Finley inquired. "Let's think about this. As the inspector said, we have been connected, although tenuously, to two deaths."

"Three, if you count Samantha."

"OK, three. So, is there any connection?"

"We don't know, since we didn't know any of them well."

"If we can't connect them directly, were there any people that were around us at the same time as all of these deaths? Any connection at all?"

"Now you really are clutching at straws! This is not our problem. I don't care if it was Prisha or any other woman," Whitt said. "As much as I liked Oliver and Samantha, I don't really want to get involved. We are going to end up in jail if we keep poking our noses where we are not invited."

Their food had arrived, fish with curry leaves and devilled shrimp, and Whitt put an end to the conversation. When they left the Galle Fort, the young policeman who had followed them was gone. Paul met them as they came into the lobby of Dutch House.

"Join me for a drink," he said. "I lost track of you after polo. What have you been up to?"

Finley and Whitt followed him across the street into the bar room. They were the only ones there. In fact, it appeared they were the only ones in the hotel.

After pouring Finley a glass of champagne and Whitt a glass of port, Paul joined them with his whiskey on the banquettes.

"I take it your young men have left. How ever have you been keeping yourselves busy?" he asked lightly.

Whitt silently delegated the telling of their tale to Finley, who gave Paul the *Reader's Digest* version. He sat silently, drink in hand. For a moment, Finley thought he had nodded off.

He raised his head slowly, looking first at Whitt and then at Finley. "You certainly live exciting lives," he commented.

"You sound like David! As if we bring this on ourselves," Whitt quipped, glaring at Paul over the rim of her glass.

"Not at all, but you do attract interesting situations," he said. "Look, since the inspector won't let you go too far and sitting here isn't going to be much fun, why don't you head out to Taprobane? It is within the boundaries of greater Galle, so you don't even have to say anything to the inspector."

He continued, "Have lunch or even stay the night. I'll give you the same rate and just transfer what you paid here over there."

Finley glanced at Whitt. She wasn't sure whether Whitt was even engaged in the conversation anymore. She seemed to have mentally withdrawn. *I bet she is trying to piece together these murders. She doesn't fool me. She says we have to leave it alone, but she hasn't. Little sneak.* Finley was getting ready to respond to Paul when Whitt cut in.

"We'll take you up on lunch, but we'll come back here for the evening."

"Needs to be before the tide comes in. But if you get caught, there are always boaters who will go and get you. Even at night," Paul said. "Then it's settled. You'll enjoy it. A quiet haven where nothing ever really happens."

Paul got up and headed toward the door. "I will just call and make the arrangements for you to join them for lunch. Be sure to wear sandals and something you don't mind getting wet." He was off before either sister could ask why they would get wet.

"Maybe one of your guidebooks explains," Finley said.

"Perhaps. I just don't want to get caught over there overnight. What if the place is haunted? There is black magic all around here."

"Whitt, you don't believe in that stuff, do you?"

"I have lived in Asia long enough to know that I don't have to believe it for it to be true."

"You've got a point," Finley added. "I have a healthy skepticism, but I keep an open mind. Stranger things have happened."

"Given our luck, we'll get stuck on a haunted island during a zombie apocalypse."

"Now you're being silly."

"Just watch."

They opened the door to their room cautiously, ready for another night of monkey marauding, but the room was clean, and there was no sight of any monkeys or mess.

"I guess we need to pack lightly tomorrow if we're going to have to wade in the water," Finley said after Whitt read a description of the restaurant, the island, and the unusual way to reach it.

"I'm trying to figure out which pair of shoes I can afford to have ruined," Whitt said. Finley smiled, trying to discern which algorithm Whitt would use to assess the relative value of her Kate Spades versus her Manolos.

"Maybe we should head down the hill before we leave for lunch and grab some cheap shoes that we don't care about for the walk over," Finley suggested. "We can stick a proper pair in our satchel."

"Mama always said you were the smart one," Whitt quipped, heading into the bathroom.

"She said no such thing, and you know it," Finley protested over the noise of the shower. *Now to decide which equipment to bring, and how to shove it all in one satchel.* She opened her camera bags and started to lay out her cameras, lenses, filters, and tripods.

I need to stop here and just make a decision, Finley said to herself, after emptying the first equipment bag. *Adding more to the piles isn't going to help. Besides, as Mama would say, it's not the kitchen— it's the cook.*

When she reached in to pull out the last few items, she felt the softness of a small cloth bag. She opened it to find a note and a small wad of paper wrapped around a band of silver that had been twisted into a symbol that she recognized as the Berber sign for endless time. She unfolded the note.

"If only time were indeed endless. Then I could be with you forever. To our love everlasting, even if time is not. Yours forever, Max." *Damn.*

15

THE ROAD TO TAPROBANE WINDED along the sea. The muddy brown of the previous day's water had settled into a dusky blue that morning, reflecting the bright turquoise of the sky uninterrupted by clouds. Adesh had taken them into the local market in town so that they could buy rubber shoes that could withstand a bit of sea water.

"I don't understand why they couldn't build a little causeway to connect the island to the mainland," Whitt wondered.

"I guess it makes the hotel more unique. How many times can you say that you walked on water for your lunch?" Finley teased.

"But that just makes it a once-in-a-lifetime thing. It isn't the sort of place that you just drop into for an impromptu lunch!" Whitt countered.

At several points along the shore, fishermen who were poised precariously on stilts anchored in the sea cast their lines out to the water. Looking like egrets standing on one leg, they dotted the coast, prompting tourists to pull over and snap pictures. Finley decided that with the right angle, aperture setting, and shutter speed, she could take a drive-by shot and dodge the crowds. She tested her hypothesis with a few practice shots and ended up with more than a few frames that she was pleased with.

The beach crossing to the island was undistinguished. Men in shorts and T-shirts sat in clusters, smoking and talking while sizing up each car that pulled in to see if it contained a potential customer or if it was just another group of friends that had come to shoot the breeze.

Adesh dialed the number of the hotel to alert them of Finley and Whitt's arrival. Shortly, a whisker-thin young man dressed in a bright-white jacket with gold epaulets and matching white shorts approached the car and reached for the door on Whitt's side.

"Misses Blake! Welcome to Taprobane!" the young man said. "My name is Hirun."

Adesh opened the opposite side for Finley. The sun danced on the water, shooting out rays of light with blinding accuracy. Whitt squinted into the sun, using her hand to shield her eyes. Finley stared at her sister. *Why that girl refuses to wear sunglasses is beyond me!*

Finley lowered her own shades to return the young man's greeting. "We can't wait to make the crossing. How high does the water get?"

"Right now, the tide is quite low, so it is an excellent time to journey to the island if you wish to walk. Or you can take the elephant." Hirun pointed to an elephant on the nearby shore that was draped in a mirrored, magenta blanket and jewel-encrusted headpiece. "If you are ready, we can go."

"We'll walk." Whitt started off after the hotel attendant.

Adesh handed Finley her camera bag and satchel. "I will be here in this place when you return this afternoon," he said. "No need to call before. I will be here."

The water covering the path barely reached the arch of Finley's foot. It looked like the parting of the Red Sea. Whitt was splashing her way across with Hirun at her elbow to steady her, but judging by Whitt's long strides, it wasn't needed.

Finley had strapped her camera across her so that she could balance the bag and satchel while snapping shots. She stood in the middle of the path, and then, using her wide-angle lens, she pivoted to each side so that the full gradation of the crystal, blue-green water could be captured. She grabbed a shot of the bedazzled elephant patiently awaiting a passenger, decided against a ride, and instead strode across the short distance of water.

"That was kind of fun. I don't know what I expected, but it wasn't that." Finley climbed the gangplank that led from the water to the stone entry path of the hotel. Built in the 1920s by an eccentric count, the hotel had only five rooms but offered lunch to short-term guests who wanted a bucket-list experience.

"I got pretty wet. Glad we have swimsuits on under this," Whitt said.

"The sun'll dry us in short order, I'm sure." The hem of Finley's skirt was already starting to stiffen as the salt from the water dried and encrusted the material.

"Ladies, how did you enjoy your walk?" The concierge, an older gentleman named Minadha, greeted them at the top of the steep path with a cool, eucalyptus-infused towel and a glass of gingered coconut water.

"Refreshing and unusual," Whitt said.

"Sir Paul has suggested that we do a brief tour before you take lunch, if that is all right with you?"

"That sounds lovely. Thank you," Whitt said, confirming with her sister and following Minadha. "How many other guests have come over for lunch?"

"You are our only luncheon guests today. So, you have the whole island to yourselves," Minadha said as he led them through the entry hall, stopping periodically to explain a painting or unusual fact about the house and the count.

"And overnight? How many are booked to stay overnight?" Finley asked.

"Tonight, we have no one with us," Minadha said. "We don't have anyone booked until early next week. So, we eagerly await serving you today."

The hotel was decorated in classic, British-colonial style, complete with caned chairs, light-linen upholstered sofas and chairs, and dark-sandalwood furniture. The lushness of the tropical landscape complemented the interior design. Taprobane was, as previous owners like the author Paul Bowles had described it, a perfect little gem.

Minadha had taken them through the common rooms and the five upstairs suites. As he pointed out the spectacular view from one of the larger suites, Whitt moved to the window to take in the view. The large, paneled window looked out to the ocean, turquoise and deep. The island itself seemed to recede, leaving a tiny rock in an endless sea.

As she turned to leave, Whitt caught a fleeting glimpse of someone she thought she recognized.

"Finley, is that Lena?" she asked in a whisper, drawing her sister back to the window.

"Where?"

"There. In the boat," Whitt was pointing in the general direction of the shore, but to a location significantly south of where Finley and Whitt had walked across.

"I can't see it. I hear a motor, but it's out of range," Finley said. "You know I'm blind."

"Maybe now I'm seeing things," Whitt joked as she played off her frustration. *I need to stop creating drama where there is none. What would Lena be doing in a small boat in the middle of the bay? She couldn't have been coming from here. Minadha says we are it for guests.*

Minadha's soft lilt brought Whitt back to the present. "You have now seen all that there is here in Taprobane. We are only 1 hectare, a bit over 2 acres in your terms. But we put a lot into our tiny package."

He led them back downstairs to the dining room. "The chef has prepared a special lunch for you, at Sir Paul's direction. I hope it will meet your approval."

He directed them to their table, which overlooked the water. After seating them, he bowed slightly and left. Soon, dish after succulent dish was coming to the table—tuna carpaccio, followed by crab curry and grilled prawn with long beans, an eggplant side, and an array of sambals, pickles, and chilies.

Finley and Whitt ate slowly so that they didn't run out of stomach before the parade of dishes stopped. Luckily, dessert was a platter of tropical fruits and ices.

"I don't think I have ever been this close to popping before," Finley said, hands resting contently on her belly.

"I know the feeling," Whitt added. "Paul outdid himself. I am afraid to take off my skirt and see myself in this bathing suit. I'll look like I'm pregnant."

"Are you?" Finley kidded.

"No more than you are," Whitt shot back with a sly smile.

"Maybe some coffee will flatten our stomachs so we aren't embarrassed sunbathing."

"No one else is here, so what do we care?" Whitt said, sipping her champagne.

They had her Pol Roger on the wine list, so Whitt asked for two bottles to be iced—one for lunch and one for later. The water looked so inviting that she was looking forward to an after-lunch dip in the infinity pool that sat on the cliff facing the ocean. She would ask that the other bottle be brought out to the poolside. *We can finish that for sure before we head back to shore. A nice, leisurely afternoon in the sun. Even the evil inspector can't ruin that.*

"I could get used to this." Finley joined Whitt in her reverie, staring out at the expanse of water and feeling as if there was no one else for miles.

"Do you think Paul would sell this island to us?"

"For the right price, I think Paul would sell his own mother," Finley laughed. "You ready for a swim?"

"Sure, although I think it will be closer to a soak and a bake in the sun."

They pushed back from the table and headed to the changing room. The room, which was part of the spa, was perfumed with the sweetness of frangipani cut by the citrus of lemongrass. An attendant handed them thick, deeply piled white beach towels as they slid open the bamboo door to the pool.

The octagon-shaped manse that housed the hotel sat on the crest of the craggy island. The pool was nestled into a leafy cliff terrace just below the restaurant. Teak-wood decking alternated with sand under the row of blue-and-white deck chairs that surrounded the pool. The glacial serenity of the water, whose edge seemed to drop into the sea, contrasted with the crashing waves below.

"Is the water getting rougher or is it just me imaging things?" Whitt asked.

"It does seem like more waves have kicked up, but the tide is also higher. Minadha said we didn't have to hurry. We could take the elephant back or send for one of the boats."

They both slid into the water and waded to the far edge where they stood for several minutes, mesmerized by the expanse of blue. From that vantage point, all that was in front of them for miles was ocean.

"Now I'm ready for my bake," Whitt said and pulled herself out of the water. She toweled off and stretched out on a nearby lounge chair.

The sisters had fallen into a food-induced stupor, so they didn't hear the waiter when he brought the champagne bucket and flutes. But they did hear the attendant when he called their names.

"Misses Blake! There is a storm blowing in. We suggest you come into the hotel now." He was gathering up their towels while the waiter hurriedly picked up the glasses and ice bucket.

The sky was a bruised gray in places, as the sun played peekaboo behind a line of thunderheads.

"Where did that come from?" Whitt asked, looking out at the horizon.

"Don't know, but it looks like we may be here for a while," Finley knew that most storms in the tropics came and went before you could get out your umbrella. But this didn't look your run-of-the-mill shower, either. Since the attendant had called them in, the wind had picked up, tossing palm fronds about the grounds.

Inside, staff had begun to stack chairs carried in from outside. Other attendants pulled in and locked the shutters. The orderly bustling brought to Finley's mind a ship's crew being ordered to batten down the hatches.

"We apologize, but this type of storm is unusual and came up very quickly," Minadha said when they returned from changing back into their street clothes. The concierge had brought their champagne, as well as a tea cart laden with cakes and scones into the elegant interior sitting room.

He continued, "It appears the storm will be with us well into the evening. We have made up a room for you upstairs. We hope you will be comfortable. At the very least, you will be safe."

The wind tried to disabuse him of that notion by whistling loudly through the palms and throwing torrents of rain against the shutters. The waving fronds on the shutters made an eerie scratching sound.

"Thank you for your hospitality," Finley said. "Had we known there was going to be a storm, we would have headed back earlier."

"I doubt even the forecasters knew about this one," Minadha said. "Very strange. But it will pass by morning, I am sure. In the meantime, please enjoy your tea."

Whitt sat across from her sister on the sofa. The waiter had set places for them and had moved the tiered cake plate and teapot over to the massive coffee table that separated the sisters.

"I guess we'd better call Adesh and let him know that we aren't coming back tonight," Whitt had pulled out her phone and was dialing his number.

"I hope he found a safe place to wait," Finley said, her brow furrowed. "That beach wouldn't be safe now."

"No service. Damn!" Whitt was checking her settings to see what was wrong. "Maybe we can see if Minadha can get through to him."

"We can see. If not, I think he'll get the idea. All we can do is wait it out," Finley said. "And eat cake!"

"I wonder if they have T-shirts we can buy to sleep in," Whitt said, before turning to the champagne and tea the staff had poured for her.

"Besides the storm, I really could get used to this!" Finley smiled as she bit into a piece of lemon tart.

"As long as this place isn't haunted, and this wasn't a diabolical plot by Paul to do away with us!"

"You really do have a vivid imagination," Finley joked. "Let's just enjoy ourselves and deal with the rest in the morning."

"If we live so long!"

By the time they were ready for bed, Finley and Whitt had sworn that the staff had been trying to clean out the wine cellar and kitchen larder. There had been so much food and wine at dinner that the sisters were looking for more guests to arrive or the staff to sit down and join them. They suspected that the staff would later dine on the leftovers, of which there were plenty.

When they arrived upstairs, they found that the hotel staff had laid out pajamas, robes, and slippers for them.

"This is a cut above our sweats and T-shirts," Finley quipped, holding up her pair of PJs.

"I'll say!" Whitt replied. "Do you think they keep a stock of nighties just in case, or are these something some rich person left behind?"

"Well, they match, so I guess it is stock they have just in case."

"These are nice. Very soft. Do you think we can keep them?" Whitt asked.

Finley had carried her pair of nighties into the bathroom, where she found toothbrushes, hairbrushes, razors, and scrunchies laid out on the vanity. When she finished her shower and slid into bed, she found Whitt still trying to connect to the internet.

"I can't even read!" Whitt pouted.

"Just give up and go to bed!"

Within thirty minutes, the lights were off, and both sisters were sound asleep.

When Finley awoke to head to the bathroom, she instinctively went to flick on the light and found that they weren't working. She tried all the switches to be sure she hadn't just blown a bulb and found that none of them worked, either. It was the storm.

Instead of going back to bed, she slipped into her robe, grabbed her camera bag, and started for the door.

"Where are you going at this time of night?" Whitt was awake and sitting up in bed.

"Sorry I woke you," Finley answered. "I thought I might try to get some shots of the lightning now that the wind has died down. I have a flashlight."

"Well, you may have a flashlight, but I don't," Whitt said. "You're not leaving me."

Whitt pulled on her robe and slippers and followed Finley out into the hall. They tiptoed down the stairs and into the hallway that ran the length of the house.

"Where are you going? All the windows are boarded up."

"The big picture window in the dining room doesn't have shutters, so I can shoot from there," Finley said. "If I angle it right, there shouldn't be any reflection."

The night sky lit up with the next crack of lightning.

"That's close!" Whitt jumped back as the flash illuminated the room followed by a sharp crack.

"Let me get a few shots, and then we can head back upstairs."

Finley directed the flashlight to her camera as she adjusted the settings and secured the filter. When the next streak of lightning flashed across the sky, Finley was ready. She clicked several shots in quick succession as multiple bolts cracked through the sky.

"We need to go upstairs. That's too close."

Finley stepped away from the window and detached her lens. She carefully returned it to the case and was zipping it up when she heard knocking.

"What's that?" Finley asked, turning to her sister.

"I don't know. I heard it too. Let's get out of here."

Finley listened, trying to place both the sound and the direction. She followed along the wall with her flashlight until the beam reached a set of stairs toward the back of the house. She listened again but heard nothing.

"Finley, this place is haunted. I told you. Let's go upstairs. Now!"

At the last word, the knocking started again. Closer now than before. Finley again pointed the light in the direction of the sound.

"It's coming from in there," Finley whispered.

"Finley, let's go!" Whitt said, but it was too late.

Finley had fixed the beam of light on a small wooden panel that ran underneath the stairs. The sound was coming from there. A knocking and a muffled moan. She crouched down near the panel, running her hand along the ridge, trying to find an opening.

"Finley, don't!"

Finley pushed hard on the wood near the top of the panel. She stepped back quickly as it sprang open. The knocking stopped. The moan was low and very near. She jerked the light toward the sound, ready to sacrifice her camera and lenses if she needed to use her bag as a weapon to defend herself and her sister. She expected a stowaway or even an animal.

What she didn't expect was Evans.

16

THE MAN IN FRONT OF them was barely recognizable. The left side of his face was swollen so that his eye was a slit encrusted with yellow ooze. He had managed to position himself in the under-stair cupboard to allow his long legs to stretch forward, but that had meant his body was folded in half against the sloping ceiling.

It was from this position that he had apparently kicked against the paneling. Shoe prints marked the door. His hair was matted with blood and dust. His hands were bound behind him, his feet roped together, and his mouth gagged and taped. He had seemingly exhausted his last reserve of energy. His head lolled on his chest, which almost rested on his knees.

"Good God! What happened?" Whitt cried. "Is he still breathing?"

She peered over her sister, who had dropped to her knees and was trying to pull Evans out of the dark cubbyhole. Every time she moved him, he winced and moaned under his gag, his eyes shut, his head still rolling from side to side.

"Barely. Hard to say what happened. We need to get him out of here to a more comfortable place so we can see how badly hurt he is."

"Where are we going to take him where he won't be found?" Whitt said. "Clearly he isn't supposed to be here. I don't know who to trust anymore!"

Finley nodded, pulling gently on Evans's shirt to fully extract him from his confinement.

"I saw a closet or storeroom down the hall. Go see if it is empty. We can put him in there until we figure out what to do," Finley whispered.

Whitt returned shortly. "It's locked."

"Watch him."

"What are you going to do? Don't break it or it will be obvious something was done."

"Trust me. They will never know." Finley said, reaching to pull a pin out of her hair. *Longer hair does have some benefits. In emergencies, at least.*

When she came back, Whitt had stabilized Evans's head in her lap. She sat cross-legged on the floor with her back against the wall.

"I think he blacked out."

"Yeah. I think he has internal injuries. Maybe a broken rib." Finley said. "I hope nothing more than that. There was very little blood in there. Maybe he was hurt elsewhere and brought here."

She knew the hard rain would have washed away any evidence of where he had been worked over. At this point, it didn't matter. They needed to keep him hidden until they could find a way to get him off the island and to a doctor.

"Help me move him. Quietly," Finley said. She had grabbed his legs, still bound together, and nodded for Whitt to take his head and shoulders.

Whitt slid her legs from under Evans and pulled herself up. They gently lifted his body and partially dragged him down the hall to the closet. He was a deadweight, so progress was slow.

"How'd you do that?" Whitt asked, motioning to the closet door which stood wide open.

"Hidden talents," Finley smiled. "I'll go in first. Once we get him in, we need to find something to cut these ropes so he can rest more comfortably."

They had just stretched Evans out in the small storeroom when they heard movement in the front of the hotel. Whitt stepped in behind her sister and quietly pulled the storeroom door closed. Finley cut the beam and put the darkened flashlight in her robe pocket. The steps neared the back stairs and then diverted through the kitchen to the other side of the house.

"The night watchman making his rounds. Did we close the cubbyhole door?" Whitt asked, as Finley turned on the flashlight again and checked on Evans.

His broad chest rose and fell with steady, but shallow breathing. His face twisted in pain from time to time. Had his mouth been free, he may even have cried out, but the gag stifled any sound he might have made.

"I'll go check that we didn't leave anything open or moved," Finley whispered, feeling for her camera bag and equipment. "Can you make it to the kitchen and grab a knife?"

The two slipped off to their respective tasks. When Finley scanned the back-stair area with her light beam, she was glad she had returned to check. She had dropped her lens cap in her effort to move Evans. She wondered whether whoever had done this might also have overlooked something, but that would have to wait until daylight.

Whitt had already cut the ropes that tied Evans's legs and was working on those behind his back when Finley returned, dragging a white sheet.

"What are you going to do with that?" Whitt looked up from hacking at Evans' restraints.

"I think his ribs are broken. While we have the knife, let's cut it into strips and wrap his chest and stomach."

"You just want to undress the man while he can't protest," Whitt said under her breath. She had broken through the straps on his wrists and was starting to cut the sheet into several long bandages.

"We don't need to undress him, fool!" Finley retorted. "His shirt is dirty, but he doesn't appear to have any wounds that could get infected. Let's just bind him until we can get him to a doctor."

"And how are we going to do that?" Whitt asked rhetorically.

"We'll figure that out later. Shut up and cut for now."

Evans was unconscious. Despite the binding, which would have been tortuous, he barely registered pain. Finley and Whitt alternated holding him up and wrapping the strips around him. Finley gently lowered him down after pulling the last strip into a knot. She placed the remaining wadded sheet under his head. She was afraid to try to tend to his swollen eye and face. Instead, she gingerly moved a chock of hair from his forehead. *He must be in so much pain. It's better that he blacked out. What in the hell happened?*

"That's all we can do tonight," Finley said. "Let's lock up and pray that he makes it through the night." She used her hairpin to reengage the lock on the door before leading her sister up the stairs to their room.

"So how are we going to move him from there without anyone seeing us?" Whitt asked when the door to their room was secured.

"We need to get back to the mainland and ask Adesh to get us a boat. The rest we are going to have to play by ear," Finley said.

"Even if we have a boat, we can't lift him down to the water." Whitt had crawled into bed. The electricity was still off so they talked by the light of Finley's flashlight.

"I know, I know. But we can't leave him here to die," Finley voice had gotten thin with emotion as she thought of Evans lying helpless in the dark storeroom.

"We'll think of something," Whitt said. "Let's get some sleep and see what we can figure out in the morning."

When they woke a few hours later, the only evidence of the angry storm was the debris left behind: myriad palm fronds, a few bushes stripped of flowers, and some overturned planters. The sky was a welcoming blue that matched the sea.

The sisters quickly showered and dressed, stuffing the only evidence of their adventure the previous night—their pajamas—in Finley's camera bag. After breakfast, they thanked the staff and waded through the shallow water to shore.

"I hope Adesh is waiting for us," Finley said as they walked across the dampened sand.

"Wonder where he stayed. With all these trees, even the car wouldn't have been safe."

"Ma'am! Ma'am!" Adesh's voice cut through the chatter of the men on the beach. He rushed over to retrieve Finley's camera equipment.

"Adesh! Are you well?" Finley asked. "You weren't here all night, were you?"

"No, ma'am. I saw the storm coming and knew you couldn't make it back, so I went to my cousin's. I tried to call you, but there was no connection."

"We tried to reach you, as well," Whitt responded. "As long as you are safe."

Finley and Whitt waited until they were in the car before they explained to Adesh their dilemma.

"He's a big man. We struggled to move him a short distance last night. There is no way we can get him down the cliff, even with three of us," Whitt said.

"And is there even a boater here that has a boat big enough to carry all of us?" Finley asked.

"Let's go away from here, and then we will try to solve this," Adesh said, backing the car out and turning down the road, away from Galle. After a short distance, he pulled the car over and began talking on the phone in Sinhala.

"My cousins will help us," Adesh explained as they waited on the side of the road. Some minutes later, a car passed and Adesh pulled out to follow behind it.

"My cousins."

The car turned into a beach a few miles down from the Taprobane landing. Several boats were anchored in the small lagoon. Three men emerged from the car, greeted Adesh, and made their introductions to Finley and Whitt before moving off toward the water.

They waded out to two small boats and started the motors. One of the boats headed out of the lagoon into the ocean while the other headed toward a larger working vessel moored some distance away.

"My cousin supplies pleasure boats and hotels with provisions and materials. So, he and his friends are known along these waters," Adesh said. "Besides, Bobo is big. And strong."

The young man was larger in stature than some of the other men the sisters had seen on the island, but he still was not Evans's size. Whitt's brow furrowed in doubt, but she held her tongue. *What other option do we have?*

With Bobo on his boat, the small dinghy returned for Adesh, Whitt, and Finley. Whitt had stashed her satchel in Adesh's car, but Finley had brought her camera bag as cover in case they were discovered in the hotel again. She wasn't sure what kind of story she would tell, but she would think of something. Her hope was that they could get on and off Taprobane without any trouble.

Adesh explained that one of Bobo's friends had gone ahead, acting as a worker arriving to do repairs. He would moor his boat, enter the grounds, and then stand ready to help Bobo carry Evans. As it turned out, that wasn't necessary.

Adesh had had the third boatman pull into a cove on the backside of the island, almost under the pool. He had gotten out and followed Finley up a steep path to the rear of the house. The boatman and Whitt had stayed behind. Whitt had accepted the plan under protest.

Finley could see Bobo's boat bobbing in the cove, but not Bobo. She led Adesh to the top of the path and headed toward the house. She hadn't decided whether she would enter through the spa or the service door. Bobo's sudden entrance from one of the alternate paths decided for her. He carried a large tarp as he strode toward the service entrance. She and Adesh followed.

Without speaking, she indicated their intended direction. She listened for sounds of any movement. There was activity in the kitchen, but besides that, the rest of the house was quiet. She led Bobo and Adesh to the storeroom, pulled a pin from her hair and popped the lock. Evans was there, in pretty much the same position that she had left him. She could hear his breath, somewhat labored now.

"We have to get him to a doctor. Now!" Finley whispered.

In one swift movement, Bobo covered Evans with the tarp and lifted him on his shoulder. Without stopping, he headed back the way they had come and toward his boat. Finley checked the dank storeroom to be sure nothing had been left and then headed toward the cubbyhole. *Maybe there is something here that will tell us what this is all about. If he di—if he doesn't make it, we are going to have to piece this together ourselves.*

Finley opened the under-stair panel and used her flashlight to scan the area. She looked for anything—a note, a button, something—that would give her answers. She saw nothing. She pushed the panel closed and stood up.

"Let's go," she mouthed to Adesh. Her eyes ran over the area one last time. *Want to be sure we don't leave anything behind, either. That inspector would love to tie us to this if anything happens to Evans.*

By the time Finley and Adesh got back to the dinghy, the other boats had disappeared. Whitt and the third boater sat in silence, waiting.

"What took you so long?" Whitt whispered angrily.

Finley smiled at her sister and touched her hand. *God, she sounds like Mama when she is worried. Looks like her, too.*

"Had to be sure we hadn't dropped anything last night," Finley shouted over the engine noise. The boat was already out of the cove and into the bay.

In no time, the boat had motored back into the lagoon. The car in which Bobo and the two boaters had arrived was pulling out onto the road. A third car took its place, and a young woman stood beside it.

"Bobo said he would meet you at the house." She greeted Adesh and the third boater in Sinhala as Finley and Whitt came ashore. She then turned to speak to the sisters in English. "I am Anu, Bobo's wife."

Adesh followed Anu's car onto the road and into a small village not far from where the boats were anchored. Finley and Whitt recognized Bobo's car, which had been pulled into the back of a house not far from the road.

"This is my aunt's house. She is good with medicines. I didn't think you wanted to go to a hospital," Adesh said.

Finley and Whitt hadn't thought that far. They hadn't considered that whatever happened, Evans wouldn't want his cover blown. They just knew that they didn't want him to die, and in his current condition, that was a real possibility.

"Thanks for thinking of that," Finley said.

Finley had explained to Adesh, when they first got ashore, how they had come to know Evans. She appreciated the trouble Adesh had gone through to help the Interpol inspector. Regardless of their perception of the police, his whole family was now involved in the effort to save Evans.

There were at least seven people crammed into the sitting room of the house when Finley and Whitt walked in. Introductions were made, and then they were led into a small bedroom near the rear of the house. Evans had been laid on the bed, the tarp thrown to the floor beside him. A petite, middle-aged woman was cutting his shirt and the bindings from his chest. She looked up, scowling when the sisters walked in.

"Did you do this?" she pointed to the sheet strips.

"Yes, we didn't know what else to do to help him," Whitt said defensively.

"At least you didn't wrap it too tight," the woman said. "He needs to breathe, or his lungs will fill with fluid. A faster death than a few broken ribs."

"Will he be OK?" Finley asked. Her eyes moved from Evans's battered face to his broad, smooth chest. Her breath seized for a moment, and she had to check herself. She prayed that Whitt hadn't seen her reaction. *What was that? You've seen a man's chest before. Why are you getting so flustered?*

"He may live, but someone was hoping that he wouldn't," the woman said. "You don't beat someone like this by accident."

She continued, "It seems that he was drugged or tied up when they did it. No defensive wounds on his hands. You don't beat a man this big and strong without him getting some licks in."

"You seem to know a lot about this. Are you a nurse?" Whitt asked, curious about the woman's background.

"A forensic pathologist back in the States," the woman responded. "Burlington, Vermont. I am Lita, by the way. Adesh's aunt."

She smiled at Adesh and said something to him in Sinhala.

"You were working, so I didn't want to interrupt," Adesh replied. "This is Misses Finley and Whitt Blake, my clients during their stay in our country."

"Is this your boyfriend?" Lita's eyes zeroed in on Finley.

"No! A friend. He helped us out in Morocco," Finley was surprised at Lita's directness. And the implication.

Lita gave Finley a half-smile. She stood, gathering up the bindings and tarp as she moved toward the door. She signaled for Adesh to follow her.

"He'll decide if he wants to get better or not. He may have internal injuries, but without an MRI or CAT scan, it is difficult to know," she said as she left. "Rest is the best medicine for a beating."

Whitt followed Lita with her eyes when she left the room.

"That's reassuring. Not," Whitt said.

"It's true, though. There isn't much else she can do for him. Except provide him a safe place to recover."

"I guess," Whitt said. "But it doesn't mean I have to like it."

"Maybe we should get Adesh to take us back to Galle. Evans will be out for a while, and we can get some rest while we can. He may need our help when he wakes up."

"If he wakes up," Whitt whispered under her breath.

17

HE'S AWAKE. IN 15 M. was all the message from Adesh said. Finley and Whitt assumed that meant that he would come with the car in fifteen minutes, but they weren't wholly sure. They had been up for several hours, had had breakfast, and had chatted with Paul about the trip to Taprobane and the storm. They had been too tired the previous evening to socialize, ordering bourbons and dinner in their room after a long soak and a nap.

Paul had obviously been briefed by his Taprobane staff, so the sisters had been circumspect in their account of the night on the island. They mentioned nothing of their return to the island the next morning or the "package" they carried away with them when they left.

When Adesh arrived, they were waiting in the lobby. Finley carted her camera bag with her to ward off questions about their destination. She also hoped to go through her pictures at some point to see if she had captured anything that might help them figure out who besides them had been on the island.

"Have a nice day touring, ladies," the concierge said as they headed to the car.

Adesh waved to the young woman as he pulled out of the gate and into the narrow street that led to town. Once through town, he headed along the sea road. Only then did he speak.

"He made it through the night. Auntie says she isn't sure how. She thinks he has some internal bleeding, but I guess it isn't too bad."

"Can he be moved to a hospital?" Whitt asked. "He sounds pretty bad off."

"If we move him to a hospital or even a clinic, there will be questions," Adesh said.

"And the inspector would love to force us to answer them. From behind bars," Finley added. "He's better off where he is until we can find Taylor or whoever else is working with him."

"Maybe he is lucid enough to give us at least that."

Evans's face was still swollen and was starting to turn a bluish purple. His eye was now covered with a white patch of cloth that had been taped to his face. His face was shaven, and someone put him into a clean white shirt. Despite all that, he still looked like hell.

Whitt stood at the side of the bed, surveying his injuries. As she lifted his hand, his good eye popped open. He relaxed when he saw who it was, and a crooked smile curled his lip.

"Looks like I can't get away from you two." His words were slurred and slow, but the voice was still resonant, even with the raspiness. "And heaven knows I do try."

"How are you feeling?" Finley said. "You had us worried."

Evans turned his head slowly to fix his gaze on Finley and Adesh, who waited at the foot of the bed.

"Who's he?" Evans asked, motioning with his head. "I've only seen a woman go in and out. More importantly, what are you do-ing here?" His words were now halting as if the effort to get them out had exhausted him. He closed his eyes. Whitt thought he had drifted off to sleep. Finley waited.

"Evans, if you are awake, just nod and we'll start talking," she said.

He nodded and Finley signaled Whitt to begin. Her version of the facts was slightly embellished but gave him enough of the story to fill him in. As she spoke, Whitt mentally stashed her questions to the side. Soon, she felt like her brain had more questions than answers, and she started peppering Evans from the stash.

"What are *you* doing here, is the bigger question? And what happened? How'd you end up on Taprobane?" Whitt asked.

Evans opened his eyes for a moment, tilted his head at Adesh and asked, "Can he be trusted?"

"He's the one that brought you off the island. Yes, he can be trusted. As can his family," Finley said.

Evans closed his eyes again and continued. "I'm working on an industrial espionage case. Large-scale. Multi-country."

"They kill people for industrial secrets?" Finley asked. "They clearly wanted you dead."

Evans smiled slightly, "Glad they didn't succeed. But yes. In pharma, defense, and biotech, there are secrets worth killing for."

"How long have you been here? And why here?" Whitt asked.

"Got here about a month ago. We've had several agents here and elsewhere worldwide trying to piece this together. It's more complex—and more dangerous—than we first had imagined."

He paused to catch a breath before starting again, "I don't know who I have left from my team. Taylor's somewhere, along with a few other men and women. Hope they've blended into the landscape here. Got to keep out of sight."

"Can't you contact them?" Finley asked.

Adesh had brought in chairs for Whitt and Finley before leaving and closing the door. The sisters pulled the chairs closer to the bed so that they could hear Evans without him having to project. His voice came in whispers. *I don't know if it's his lungs or his ribs, but he is struggling to breathe. This can't be good.*

"I don't know who to trust. Afraid to expose them…" Evans had left the rest of the thought hanging. He had drifted back to sleep. His breathing was slow, but steady. Finley watched his chest rise and fall, mesmerized by the rhythm and afraid that it would stop at any minute.

"Let's go into the other room," Whitt said. She had moved her chair to the wall and was at the door.

"I'll be out in a minute." Finley said, her eyes fixed on Evans's face.

Whitt nodded and closed the door behind her. The room was quiet. Finley could hear the murmur of voices in the outer room and movement in the courtyard outside the window, but the room itself felt sealed, protected. She lifted Evans's hand and held it. His long, elegant fingers had not been marred the way his face had. His palm was warm and twitched slightly when she touched it.

She wondered why she was there. What was it that made her want to silently assure him that he was not alone? In the hushed, whitewashed room, she sat and held his hand in hers, her breathing paced to his. Not moving. Not talking. Just communicating. His eyes were still closed when she placed his hand on his stomach and stood to leave.

"Find Taylor," Evans said. Finley stilled.

"I will," she promised and closed the door shut.

"You OK?" Whitt asked when Finley walked into the sitting room. Adesh and his cousins were in the courtyard, talking in Sinhala. Finley couldn't understand the conversation, but it was animated. She knew they were the likely topic.

"What's going on?" Finley nodded at the group outside.

"They are trying to figure out next steps," Whitt said. "Some of them are concerned about him staying here too long. They don't want problems with the police."

"Are they afraid he's going to die on them?"

Whitt paused, "He might. He's pretty bad off, according to Adesh."

"What is his aunt saying?"

"She says to leave him for another day or so. If there is internal bleeding, he'll probably decline in the next few hours. If not, he'll just need time to heal."

"If he gets worse, we'll take him to the hospital. I'll deal with the inspector myself, then. Adesh can call us another cab so that his family is not involved," Finley said.

"I'm with you," Whitt said. "Let's see if we can just hang here for a while and see how he does."

Lita came from the kitchen with a pitcher and three glasses. "Watermelon juice. Want some?"

"Yes, please," Whitt said. "I didn't realize how thirsty I was."

"The salt from the water dries you out." She poured three glasses of juice. "Anu should be back soon. I sent her to the market to shop for dinner. I hope you will join us."

"We don't want to impose," Whitt said.

"Any more than we already have," Finley added. "You and your family have been most generous helping us and our friend. We don't want to cause trouble."

"Who is he?" Lita asked quietly. "Why does Adesh not want to go to the hospital?"

Finley gave Lita some background on the sisters' relationship with Evans. Without saying Interpol, Lita understood that he was some kind of cop and was in trouble. That was enough for her.

"The boys can debate all they want, but he can't be moved for a couple of days at best." Lita didn't say whether Evans would be dead or alive when they moved him. She didn't have to. Finely and Whitt had started to internalize the severity of his condition.

"He may have a friend, a colleague on the island. If we can find him, he may be able to get him out of here so he can get some help," Finley said.

"Well, for now, let him rest," Lita said. She cast a glance at Finley, "He's a handsome one, even with that eye!"

Finley smiled. Lita was determined to pair her off with Evans. It wasn't a bad ordering—it just wasn't the right one. She had Max. But Lita didn't know that, nor did she need to.

"Do you girls cook? Or are you modern ladies?" Lita asked as Anu came in with a bag of groceries.

"We're from the South. We can bring home the bacon *and* fry it up!" Whitt let her low-country drawl slip in softly.

Lita laughed heartily and waved them into the kitchen. Being invited into a woman's kitchen was an honor that the sisters understood. Over the next few hours, the four women chopped and sliced, sautéed, and fried. Adesh had come in at some point to check on the sisters and found them aproned, sweating, and laughing with the other women in the kitchen area. *However liberated we are, there is something comforting about the sisterhood of women in a kitchen.*

At regular intervals, Lita, Finley, and Whitt took turns monitoring Evans. He appeared to be sleeping soundly. Probably the best that could be hoped for. When the meal had been prepared, Lita called the men into the kitchen and sent them out again with plates and glasses to set the large wooden table in the green of the courtyard. Lita, Anu, Finley, and Whitt followed with pots of curry, rice, and vegetables. Bobo and Adesh had laid out banana leaves, mounded with crispy grilled fish and large prawns.

"That's what you were doing out here," Finley said, pointing to the smoking half-barrel that served as the grill. "I wondered what you were all clustered around."

"This smells so good." Whitt was eyeing the fish and shrimp. "Do you eat like this all the time?"

"It isn't much," Lita said. "You should see when we have weddings. We cook and eat for days! But we are glad to welcome you into our house."

The meal was celebratory, even under the circumstance that brought them together. A tub holding cans of Lion beer was shoved under the table. From time to time during dinner, a can would appear at one end of the table and its empty brother would be pushed into a bucket at the other end. Whitt raised an eyebrow at Finley, who simply shrugged. *Who knows how many they had. Maybe it was better that way. At least until you go to empty the bucket!*

The table had been cleared of dinner and new leaves were laid out that held slices of fruit. The men had taken the tub of beer that had miraculously been refilled and headed to a firepit that had been dug in the garden.

Bobo layered it with wood and dried fronds and set it alight. The day was still early, but the heavy midday meal had led most of the group to nap on the lawn. The smoky fire would keep the bugs away while they slept.

The four women took time to sit at the table and enjoy their dessert. Talk was sparse, but the connection was strong. *This feels like it does at home. Women cooking and talking so much that eating is an afterthought until you sit your weary bones down and savor.*

"You're smiling to yourself. What are you thinking?" Lita was looking at Finley. Behind the laser focus was a smile that caused her eyes, instead of her mouth, to turn up at the corners.

"About how much this is like home in South Carolina," Finley finally said. "How women bond over food. Doesn't matter the country. Food connects without words."

"True. Food and crisis," Anu said. "Women know how to make the most out of both."

"Speaking of which, it is your turn to check on the patient, Finley," Lita said. Finley rose and headed into Evans's room. He was awake when she walked in.

"What's going on out there?" His voice was stronger, and his words came faster.

"Dinner. You hungry?" Finley asked. "We made some soup that you might be able to keep down."

"Soup? That's all I get?" Evans said. His smile was twisted by his swollen face.

"I suppose we can put some meat or fish in it. I'll have to ask Lita. But that you are hungry is a good sign."

"How long have I been here?"

"Only a couple of days, but I don't know how long you were on the island," Finley said. Evans said nothing. He was focused on something that Finley couldn't see. His mind only came back into the room when Finley headed toward the door.

"Let me get you something to eat, and then I'll go find Taylor," Finley said. "Any idea where to start looking?"

"He was playing tourist at a hole-in-the-wall place in Galle Fort. My head is too jumbled to think of the name now." Evans grimaced as he tried to straighten himself in the bed.

"Just sit still. You're going to unsettle something with all that moving," Finley said. "I'll get Lita."

She found Lita in the kitchen. Finley could hear Anu and Whitt outside, laughing about something.

"He's awake. And hungry." Finley moved toward the stove. "Can he have some of the soup?"

"Leave it to a man to worry a woman gray, and then wonder what she has on the stove for him to eat!" Lita said lightly. "I'll put some fish in it for him. We'll see if he can stomach it."

She spooned rice into a bowl and then topped it with broth and vegetables before crumbling in leftover grilled fish.

"Are you feeding him, or shall I?" Lita held out the bowl.

"I'll let you do it," Finley smiled at Lita's continued attempt at matchmaking. "I am going to see if Adesh can drive us back into town so we can try to find his colleague."

"He will be fine here," Lita said. "If he was going to die, he would have done so already." Finley gasped. She had rarely heard someone talk so directly or so neutrally about death.

"I'm sorry if I shock you," Lita laughed softly. "I have dealt with death so often, I guess I am immune to the associated pain. In any case, I will keep him safe."

Finley thanked her and headed into the yard. Adesh and Bobo were talking while the other men sprawled out on the grass around the pit.

"Would it be possible to take us back into town? Lita says Evans is OK here for now," Finley said. "I need to try to find his friend, so he can get him out of here."

Adesh rose and hugged his cousin while Finley headed to the courtyard to collect Whitt. With goodbyes and thank-yous

174

said, Adesh turned the car toward Galle. Once inside the Fort, he dropped them at the gate.

"I will wait here for you. Call me if you need help." Adesh's forehead creased with worry. "These are not good people. They may want to hurt you, so call. Please."

Whitt touched his arm gently before heading off into the heart of the old city. When they reached the Galle Fort Hotel some three hours later, they had seen no evidence of Taylor. They had checked every two-star hotel in the guidebook and started on the list of three-stars.

"Hopeless. Absolutely hopeless." Whitt had settled into one of the large leather chairs in the lobby of the hotel. Finley signaled for a waiter while Whitt texted Adesh.

"Do you want tea or a drink and snacks?"

"A drink. Snacks can come later." Whitt had leaned her head back, eyes closed. "G&T, heavy on the G and the lime."

Finley gave the waiter the order and turned her attention back to her sister.

"He's here somewhere. Evans is fine with Lita. We'll start again tomorrow to look for Taylor," Finley said. "We have a couple more days here, and if necessary, we can cut the time in Colombo short."

"I know. It's just that it's almost impossible to figure out where to start." Whitt sipped on the drink that she had nearly grabbed out of the waiter's hand before he could set it down. She drew in a deep breath, and then exhaled it in a sigh.

"Whitt, we'll figure it out. The city isn't that big."

"Big enough! It almost swallowed Evans whole. We were just lucky to have found him. And we may not be lucky twice."

18

THE MORNING YIELDED NO BETTER indications of where Taylor might be than the evening before had. They wandered around the city, stopping into hotel after hotel looking for their "friend who had lost his credit card." They described Taylor in detail and hoped that someone might recognize him, but they had no luck.

"These guys have some nerve. 'No, we have no one that matches that description,'" Whitt imitated, "'But you can leave the card with us in case he comes here.' How dumb do they think we are?"

Finley laughed at her sister's expression. It has been a trying morning, but a trip to the jewelers had captured Whitt's attention. And the promise of coffee after had gotten Finley's.

The owner of the jewelry store was excited to see Whitt. It was as much about the prospect that she would have some new commission for him as it was about her evident satisfaction with the design job he had done with the tourmaline she had purchased.

"I think I'm going to cry," Whitt sat staring at the creation made from the raw stone she had chosen. "From my crappy drawing, you conjured up this. It's gorgeous!"

The ring was indeed a beautiful piece—silver enveloping a crag of dark green, shot through with a brilliant prism of blue. The setting had left spaces for the light to hit the stone and alter the depth of its color.

"You and David outdid yourselves with that one." Finley held her sister's hand up to the light so that the sunlight could play with the stone's hues. "So, have you decided what your engagement ring is going to look like?"

"Who says we're engaged?"

"That boy would not have left here without a firm answer from you, and I know you told him something."

"Yeah, I told him yes," Whitt said, "But he has to wait until he asks Daddy."

"He told me he had already called him!"

"So, you two are talking behind my back, are you?"

"No, you were there. You just weren't listening."

"He did call Daddy, and Daddy said yes, but I want them to meet face to face," Whitt said. "What if Daddy and Mama don't like him?"

"Since when did that ever stop you?" Finley laughed, remembering all the times that Whitt had cajoled, maneuvered, or persuaded Daddy to allow her to do as she pleased.

The jeweler wanted to do some final refinements on the setting and promised to deliver the finished ring to the hotel that evening.

"I can't wait to show it to him," Whitt was still gushing about the ring as they walked toward Peddler Street so that Finley could get her coffee.

"Hello! Hello! Funny running into you two." Helen beckoned them from across the cobbled street. Richard followed closely behind her, looking somewhat troubled. Finley watched the two cross the road. Richard always seemed at one of two extremes—either frustrated by Helen's behavior or trying to calm it.

"I thought you had left already," Whitt said. "Decided you wanted another cooking lesson?"

"No. I got a tummy bug, so we had to delay our departure," Helen said.

"Hope you're feeling better now." Finley stepped back to put some space between Helen and her. *That's the last thing I need. An iffy stomach while we're trying to find Taylor and get Evans out of here.*

Helen laughed, "I'm not contagious now, I don't think. It was a couple of days ago. Where are you headed?"

"We're going for coffee. Care to join us?" Whitt offered.

"Sure. Have you tried Bono's? It's a little place we found on our wandering, isn't that right, Richard?" Helen seemed to be trying to draw Richard out of a daze. He snapped back to attention when she called his name the second time.

"Sorry. Lost in a fog. What did you say, love?" Richard asked.

"I was telling them about the little coffee shop we found in that alley when we were wandering." Helen's eyes locked with Richard's. She tilted her head slightly, almost willing him to nod in agreement. Eventually, he did.

"Oh, yes. Now I know where you mean," Richard said. "Are we headed there now?"

"If you girls are game?"

Finley looked at Whitt. Coffee was coffee to her. As long as it was strong, rich, and black. Whitt shrugged and started off behind Helen who was striding ahead. As she walked, Helen kept up a steady stream of conversation. Richard trudged along behind, pulling up the rear.

Helen's monologue continued for some fifteen minutes. By now, they were well into the old city, a spiderweb of narrow streets and alleys in a part of town to which neither Finley nor Whitt had ever been.

"How much farther?" Finely asked. "My coffee reserves are running real low."

"Not far. As I remember," Helen replied, looking back at Richard as if to confirm. He nodded in response. "Just around this corner."

When they rounded the corner, Helen stopped abruptly. Finley thought she had lost her way and had started to turn to head in the other direction. It was the look of despair melded with remorse on Richard's face that stopped her. She turned to find Helen with a gun pointed at Whitt. Whitt had not made a sound, her eyes focused on the weapon in Helen's hand.

"Just give us the key ring and no one will get hurt," Helen said excitedly. "We didn't want to do this, but they made us. Why did you have to take it? It isn't yours. Who are you, and why have you been following us?"

Whitt cast a side eye at Finley, stopping short of rolling her eyes. *Even in a crisis, Whitt has little patience for fools. I hope Helen doesn't piss her off and make her do something crazy that gets both of us killed. But I do have to concede that this chick is more unstable than I thought.*

"Helen, what is this about? We haven't been following you. We don't have a key ring," Finley said, her voice low and her words paced evenly. "Why do you think we have your key ring?"

"Richard's doesn't work and they are angry. They say you have it and we have to get it back. We have to get it back. Now." Helen was starting to get red faced. She was waving the gun around as she became more agitated.

"Helen, calm down before someone gets hurt," Richard raised his hand. "Stop moving that thing around. You're going to shoot someone."

Richard continued, directing his question to Finley. "Why did you ask me whether I still had my key ring the other day?"

"I had seen one at one of the stands and was considering getting one like it," Finley replied.

"But that's not what you said…" Richard started to speak, but Helen interjected.

"It doesn't bloody matter what she said. She has it and better bloody well give it to us!" Helen was shouting now. "Give it to me before I count to ten, or someone's going to get shot."

"Helen, that is not what we agreed." Richard was looking at his wife in shock. *If he is surprised, then someone really is going to get hurt. We need to think of something—and fast.*

"Shut up, Richard. Just shut up! You're confusing me," Helen was shaking her head in response to some unspoken question that only she had heard.

"Helen. Dearest. We don't want to hurt anyone. We just want to get our money, and then go back home," Richard said calmly.

"But we can't go home without the money, and they say we can't get the money without the key ring!" Helen screamed. "Give me the bloody key ring!"

She raised the gun and moved it back and forth between Whitt and Finley. Her voice had lowered. "One... two... three..." she counted slowly, swaying like a pendulum between the two sisters, a smile growing larger on her face. *She really is delusional She has completely lost touch with reality. That's not good. Really not good for us.*

"Helen, don't do it. Please, don't!" Richard pleaded.

"Four... five... si—" Helen never finished the last number.

From the terrace above came a hard rain of what seemed to be tiny cannon balls. In truth, they were unripe fruits. Mangoes, it seemed. Whitt and Finley ducked under the nearest veranda as the torrent continued.

Helen tottered before her bum hit the pavement, the gun flying from her hand. Richard had been hit several times in the initial barrage and lay cowering on the cobbles. From their position behind a table they had ruined over just in case bullets started flying, Finley and Whitt saw two figures drop down from the balcony above. Like Batman and Robin. In a scene from the movies, within seconds, Helen and Richard were in handcuffs and the gun recovered. Even so, neither Finley nor Whitt moved from their position.

"Are you OK?" A woman's voice asked, in concern. "Were you hit?"

"No, we're all right." Whitt raised her head above the table edge and nearly fell over in surprise. "Prisha?"

"Hi. Yes, and no. My name really isn't Prisha, but you can call me that for now," the woman said.

"We thought you were dead!" Finley joined her sister, staring at the apparition in front of them.

"Why would you think that?" asked a voice that both sisters recognized. Taylor.

"Finally. We have been looking all over for you!" Whitt rounded the table and grabbed his face. She kissed him solidly on the cheek. The young man blushed.

"What was that for?" he asked. "And why did you think Prisha was dead?"

"After the cooking class, we were taking a tour of the embankment, and a woman was pushed off. She looked like you. Same clothes, same hair," Whitt said, recalling the crumpled body on the beach.

"I had been following the Lockes after class. They met up with some people just outside their hotel, and they all had headed to the bastion." Prisha said. "I lost them after that."

"And why were you looking for me?" Taylor asked. "How did you even know I was here?"

"Evans. We were looking for you because of Evans," Finley said. "We'll explain everything later, but first, what are you going to do with them?"

Finley looked over at the Lockes who had been tied to a tree, in addition to being cuffed. They were sitting together, with Helen still arguing and Richard staring up angrily into space. Periodically, he would turn to her and say, "Shut up, Helen! Just shut up!" However, it failed to silence her.

"What's with those two?" Taylor asked. "We've been following them for weeks. Never thought they would get violent. This was a surprise."

"They said that someone told them they had to get the key ring back, or they wouldn't get their money," Whitt said. "They say we have it."

"And we do. Remember?" Finley whispered.

"Oh, my goodness. That's what they were after?" Whitt said, recalling suddenly what she had found in her backpack.

"You mentioned Evans. Where is he?" Prisha asked.

Whitt started to explain about the key ring and the monkeys and the Lockes. Before she could fill them in on Taprobane, the storm, and Evans, a police car pulled into the alley. Inspector Pinto got out.

"You again?" he said, walking purposefully toward Finley and Whitt. "I have you this time. Let me see how you are going to explain this?"

He continued, signaling to two police officers that were trailing behind. "Bring these two women in for questioning."

He turned his attention to Taylor and Prisha.

"Who are you? Part of their gang?" the inspector asked snidely.

"Interpol. Working with your national police," Taylor said, showing the inspector his badge.

"And her?" the inspector asked with a smirk. "Is she Interpol too?"

Prisha reached into her boot and pulled out her badge.

"At your service." Prisha said politely. "We called you to take in two suspects that we apprehended. Your national service will have the background. We will accompany you to file the reports."

He directed his attention to Finley and Whitt. "So, I was right about you all along," he snapped. "Murder wasn't enough. You must have done something really nasty to have Interpol brought in."

"They aren't our targets." Taylor pointed away from Finley and Whitt toward the Lockes. "They are. They are to be kept under tight security. Don't screw this up."

Inspector Pinto's eyes narrowed, locking on Finley and Whitt. "What about them?"

"What about them? I am assuming they can press charges if they like," Prisha said. "They did have a gun held on them."

"Are you sure it wasn't their gun?" the inspector pressed on.

"Yes. We are sure," Taylor said, his exasperation barely disguised. "Can you take these two to the station now? We would like to start our questioning. This is part of something larger, and time may be of the essence."

The inspector backed down. He directed the police officers, who stood on either side of the sisters, to take the Lockes to the awaiting patrol car. After words with Taylor and Prisha, he followed.

"He has it in his mind that you are part of this operation," Prisha said. "He won't let it go."

"We aren't part of anything, but we have shown up in some pretty incriminating places. When you finish your report, meet us at Dutch House and we can fill you in," Whitt said.

"And take you to Evans," Finley added.

19

FINLEY AND WHITT WERE IN the courtyard nursing their second rounds of bourbon by the time Prisha and Taylor arrived at the hotel. *We really are going to become booze hounds if we keep getting into dicey situations every time we are together. This has to stop for the sake of our livers—if not our sanity.* Finley thought.

"Can we get you something to drink? We are drinking bourbon but tell us what you would like." Whitt said rising from her chair to greet the two.

"A Coke and a water, if you don't mind," Prisha said. "We are still on duty."

"What did you learn from the Lockes, if anything?" Finley asked. "I'll bet Helen was still running her mouth, and Richard was stoic."

"In fact, it was the opposite," Taylor explained. "As soon as she got near the police station, she went as quiet as a mouse. Her husband did all the talking."

He continued, "Supposedly, they were contacted online and asked if they wanted to make a bit of money when they traveled. They got hit in the financial downturn and needed to make fast cash."

"We still don't understand exactly how this operation works, but it seems to follow the same pattern—elderly or retired people, mainly couples, get contacted and asked if they want to make some extra money," Prisha said. "They never meet their contact. It's all done via text."

Taylor added, "The Lockes story is pretty much the same as the others we have arrested. They just make a drop of whatever they are carrying when they get the message, and then the money appears in an account that was setup in their name."

"We haven't been able to trace the accounts back to any person or organization," Prisha said. "If we dig too deeply, the account disappears, and with it, all the evidence. It has been frustrating, to say the least."

"So, where is Evans?" Taylor asked. "We haven't been able to contact him for a good three to four days."

He continued, "Frankly, I feared he was dead. We have lost three agents that I know of."

"Three? How many did you start with? And who are these people that they can kill three agents without any fear of getting caught?" Whitt asked, her eyes rounded in surprise.

"We can get to that later. The real question is whether you guys are safe now?" Finley asked. "We don't want to bring Evans out of hiding if he still has a target on his back."

"Do you need to go into hiding, too?" Whitt added.

"It's been pretty quiet, at least until today," Taylor said. "We located the other two agents. And I found Prisha—or, really, she found me."

"I think we are OK," Prisha said. "But we do need to get out of here. Our cover is blown after this morning."

"We can take you to Evans, but I would suggest you arrange transportation out of here before we do that, in case you have to move quickly," Finley said. "We don't think we have been followed, but we don't know for sure."

"Good idea. If we haven't been able to find him, he's likely safe where he is," Taylor said. "Let me see what we can do for transport."

He rose and went into the garden, dialing as he went. Finley and Whitt could hear snatches of the conversation, but not enough to follow. *I really don't want to know any more than I do. These guys might have to shoot us if we know too much.* Whitt considered.

Prisha broke the silence. "There are a lot of moving pieces to this case that we still don't understand. Maybe if you can share with us your interactions with the Lockes, we might start to connect the dots."

She went on, "If Evans can read you into the case, you might be able to help us out. I'm assuming Evans is hurt. How badly?"

Whitt recounted how they found Evans and took him to his current hiding place. While she wanted to share more about his condition, she hesitated, unwilling to curse him with over-optimism only to find that he had died during the night. She looked at Finley for support.

"He's recovering pretty well, but he probably needs better medical treatment than he can get here," Finley said.

Taylor had caught the last part of the conversation. "Can he be moved?"

"He has been a couple of times," Whitt replied. "Don't know that that did him any good, but the moves were necessary. I don't think he can walk, but he should be able to be carried."

"We may have transport by tomorrow," Taylor said. "Is there a deserted beach we can use? A boat is being sent, but we have to get him on it without raising questions."

"I think that can be arranged," Finley indicated. "It might be best if we take you to him, and then we can all try to figure this out."

Adesh was in the hotel driveway less than five minutes after Whitt called him. He had been waiting in the alley up the street, keeping watch. He was still uncertain of who the good guys and the bad guys were. He was wary of the two characters with Finley and Whitt. He hadn't met them before, but the sisters didn't seem concerned.

"Did you come by fairy dust?" Whitt asked when they squeezed into the car.

"I was parked up the street," Adesh said, smiling. "It has a good view of the hotel entrance so I can watch who goes in and out. I saw these two go in and would have stopped them if you hadn't said you were expecting guests."

"These are Evans's friends," Finley said. "They are going to try to get him off the island."

Adesh glanced over at Taylor who was in the passenger seat before looking at Prisha in the rearview mirror. "You were at the cooking class, but you left before the others."

"Was I that obvious?" Prisha laughed. "I need to work on my shadowing skills."

"No, I was just keeping an eye on my clients," Adesh smiled. "They seem to attract trouble."

Whitt got ready to speak but bit her tongue. She couldn't disagree with what Adesh had said. They really did seem to be trouble-magnets every time they traveled. It was probably a good thing that they had someone like Adesh to look out for them.

Adesh pulled the car into a covered area at the back of the house. It appeared to be a workshop of some sort, full of tools and auto and machine parts.

"When you are ready to move him, you can carry him from the house to the car without being seen," Adesh said. "I wanted to check to see if anything was visible from the road if I parked here."

He led the way to the house. Lita and Anu were in the sitting room. The cousins had gone to the lagoon, ostensibly to mend nets, but more likely to drink and talk without comments from the women.

"How's the patient today?" Adesh asked after introducing Taylor and Prisha.

"He's awake. We had him walking a bit this morning," Lita said. "He tires quickly, but he seems to be healing."

She opened the door to the bedroom and found Evans sitting on the edge of the bed, getting ready to stand. He was wearing a pair of jeans and a white poplin tunic.

"Where do you think you are going?" Lita asked, her voice vacillating between anger and amusement.

"With them! I heard them when they came into the courtyard," Evans said. "I know you will be glad when I'm out of your hair."

"It's been nice to use my skills on the living for once, but if you try to stand without help, it will be a mistake," Lita said, laughing. "I should have put you in a sarong. It might have slowed you down."

Taylor interrupted before the banter went much further, "No need to rush. We can't get out of here until tomorrow at the earliest. So, save your strength."

Evans sighed, "Then what are you doing here now?"

He was starting to get grumpy, the kind of agitated restlessness felt by men of action who are forced to sit still. Finley could see that he wasn't a good patient, but she knew that Lita was more than his match.

"They need to talk to you," Finley said. "They have gaps in the picture and think we all have bits that might help them flesh it out."

Evans stared at her with his signature, hawk-like intensity. His jaw flexed a few times before his shoulders relaxed, and he turned to Taylor.

"Have you read them in yet?" Evans asked, nodding at Finley and Whitt. He looked at Lita, who was standing near the door. "Her, too."

"No need, whatever that means. All I can tell them is how much you ate and when you slept," Lita said jokingly. "I think Adesh and Bobo may know more."

Lita brought in Adesh and Bobo and closed the door behind her. She and Anu headed into the kitchen to start cooking. It was going to be a long night, and everyone in that small, whitewashed bedroom would need to be fueled. Especially the attractive inspector who had only just begun to heal.

"For me, there are two questions with a whole lot of flying pieces that haven't landed in a pattern yet," Taylor said. "We know what they are after—high-tech industrial secrets. But how do they get them, and then who are the linchpins in the system?"

Whitt had asked Lita for some paper, pens, and tape. She had started taping sheets to the wall. *Leave it to baby sis to organize this chaos. She may have to paper the whole room to untangle this mess.*

"Let's start with the how, since you have some information from the Lockes," Finley said. "Whoever it is uses older couples while they are on vacation as part of their delivery network. How many of these carriers have you talked to thus far?"

"About twenty worldwide. Those interviews led us to believe that there were going to be several exchanges here in Sri Lanka for some reason," Evans said. "That's another question—why here and why now? But let's focus on the how right now."

"OK, so have any of those interviewed ever met their contacts or who they think might be the contact?" Finley continued.

"No, it appears to all be done electronically," Taylor said. "Which leads me to believe, based on the detailed info given in the drop messages, that the contacts are either local people or are observing the couriers once they are in country."

"Is there anything that all the couriers have in common? Besides being older and retired?" Whitt asked.

"They generally were part of a tour group," Prisha said. "The Lockes—and one other couple—were an exception."

"See! I told you clumping wasn't attractive," Whitt pointed at Finley. "There have been so many tour groups on this island, and this is supposed to be the off-season."

She continued, "And they all seem to be German! I concluded that all Germans must clump. Finley said I was being prejudiced."

"It's late. Why don't you stop and grab something to eat?" Anu said. "You can bring it in here and keep working, but you won't last long without food."

She touched her husband's belly as she passed him and laughed. "I know at least one who is hanging on by a thread."

When the others filed out to get dinner to bring their food back in, Finley stayed to survey the sheets. Evans followed her with his good eye as she walked up and down the line.

"Are you starting to see a pattern?" Evans asked when she had completed what must have been her ninth or tenth rotation.

"I think so," she said quietly. She turned to face him. "What are you seeing?"

"Let's wait until the others get back. Then we can start hypothesizing."

"OK. In the meantime, what can I bring you to eat?" Finley asked. "More soup?"

Evans laughed. "No more soup, please! I'm already swimming in it. Whatever they have is fine."

Lita helped Finley carry Evans's plate back in. She arranged a napkin under his chin and laid another one across his lap.

"You get to feed yourself today," Lita chortled. "I think you've been playing injured so you can be pampered."

"You and your family have done your share in spoiling me," Evans answered, tucking into the bowl of curry rice on his tray. His face was still swollen and his eye bandaged, so his smile remained lopsided, but genuine.

The group was silent for several minutes as they savored the food Anu and Lita had prepared for them—curry rice with pickles and shredded pork. Whitt had added a few other notes on the sheets, and Finley moved in to see what had been written. The monkeys. Whitt had noted when their room had been invaded by monkeys.

"You got it!" Finley whispered to her sister. She set her plate down and started her pacing again.

"In Kandy, Nuwara Eliya, and Galle," Finley said to herself. "Where were the Lockes each time? Where were the agents each time? Where were the van Dijks? And where were the monkeys?"

Soon she and Whitt were both adding marks to the sheets. After several minutes of making revisions, Finley went to the sitting room and retrieved her camera case. She pulled both cameras from the bag and started scrolling through the frames.

"Is this your Dutch couple?" She turned the viewfinder to Evans so he could see the image.

"Yes. That's the woman," Evans said. "Do have a shot of the husband?"

Finley advanced the frames and stopped at a picture of the man she knew as Alfred.

"That's him," Evans took his time processing the image. "Do you have others of them?"

"I think so. I didn't know what I was looking for, but I may have shots of them in all of these locations," Finley said. "I may also have some shots of crowds that get you something."

She passed the camera around to the others. "Have any of you seen these two anywhere else? Maybe if we can place them on the location sequence it will help tie things together."

When the camera got to Bobo, he grunted, "I saw these people a couple of days ago when I was making deliveries. They were in a skiff. Thought it was strange. They look more like yacht folks."

"When and where did you see them?" Finley asked, looking to be sure Whitt was ready to capture the information. She could feel in her bones that it was going to be important.

"Like three days ago. The day before we came to get you," Bobo said. "I was dropping off some supplies to the kitchen at the hotel, and they came into the bay at a clip. Thought it was just some kids acting crazy but then I saw her. She didn't belong on that type of boat. Like I said, she was more of a yacht lady."

20

WE HAVE THE WHO, THE why, and part of the how, but not all of it." Taylor had taken the camera from Bobo and was flipping through Finley's pictures.

"Lena van Dijk—or whatever her name is—and her husband are responsible for trying to kill you, and most likely, killing your agents," Whitt said. "We can place her in each of the locations where someone died. And we can probably confirm when with the time stamp on the pictures."

"I can bring her in for attempted murder, if I can catch her, but I want her to take me to the top dogs in this operation," Evans said. "As much as I hate to say it, we have to hold off picking her up until we can tie her into the network."

"Let's go back, then, so we can understand how the network operates. From what the Lockes and the others said, they don't know their contact," Finley said. "So, Helen and Richard don't know Lena and Alfred as anything other than their travel friends."

She walked up to the sheets and noted what she was starting to see as a pattern.

"Let's try this out," Finley said. "It has to do with older couples as carriers, the van Dijks, the handlers or contacts or whatever you want to call them, a larger network of these carriers and handlers, and the monkeys."

"Monkeys?" Prisha asked.

"What have monkeys got to do with this?" Taylor was looking at Finley like she had grown horns.

"Everything," Whitt said. "Everything."

"I think Whitt figured it out." Finley had walked over to the sheets papering the walls. "Whitt has marked everywhere there was a monkey incident."

Whitt pointed to the stylized monkey faces she had drawn on the sheets. "There was the visit to our room in Kandy, followed by the mess the next night. Then, the shrieking chimp in Helen's room in Nuwara Eliya."

"Then we had the invasion in our room in Dutch House a few nights ago."

"So?" Taylor was straining to see the connection.

"So maybe that is how the network works," Finley said. "There are carriers who get the information. And then there are handlers who manage the carriers—tell them where to put the information."

She continued, "So that the handlers don't have to reveal themselves, they use monkeys to retrieve the packages or drives."

"I think we saw one monkey trying to retrieve a drive on a key ring. And I think we heard him being called off." Whitt described for Evans what had happened in the Lockes' room.

Finley went to her camera case and pulled a key ring drive from the side pocket.

"Richard had a key ring like this," Finley said. "This one was found in Whitt's backpack. And we saw another one that looked like it with the van Dijks.

"I've been trying to figure out how this thing works, and I think I figured it out." She turned over the ring to reveal a small sensor. "The information is on the drive and when the handler wants the device retrieved, they activate a little sensor that the monkeys follow."

"There must be something else that the monkeys are trained to look for, though, because more than once, the monkeys came and tore up the place looking for something—most likely the drive—and there wasn't anything with a sensor," Whitt added.

"Maybe the handlers always book the same rooms," Finley conjectured.

"That would make sense. Our agents in Kandy said that the Lockes left early so they missed them, and some Americans had moved into their room," Taylor said.

"That would have been us," Finley noted. "So, we know now why our room got trashed."

"But why was it trashed here?" Whitt asked.

"This may be crazy, but what if after Prisha switched the drives, the van Dijks figured it out and started looking for the fly in their ointment, so to speak," Finley said, looking at Prisha. "You said you passed it to Oliver."

"And then let's say he was being followed, and he was looking for a place to unload it," she continued.

"That place being us!" Whitt said, recalling their chance meeting with Oliver over coffee and their later discovery of the key ring in her bag.

"So, when the van Dijks figured out that Oliver didn't have it, they went looking for it in our room," Finley said.

"And when they still didn't find it, they sent the Lockes after us to get it back," Whitt concluded.

Finley turned to Evans. "There may be a few holes in the story, but it fits as good as anything else you have."

Taylor smiled, bringing the camera over to show Evans a frame on the viewfinder. "And this makes it fit a little neater."

Evans's face lit up with a lopsided grin. He looked at the frames before and after the shot that Taylor had shown him.

"Mark those, please," Evans said to Taylor. "We are going to need those pictures as evidence."

"Evidence of what?" Finley asked, leaning to look at a picture of Alfred van Dijk talking to a large, balding man smoking a fat, seemingly expensive cigar.

"Of the van Dijk's connection to the Turpov network. Turpov is serious bad news—drugs, human trafficking, trade secrets, cyber breaches, you name it," Evans said. "It may not break up their operations, but arresting some of their handlers, for even a short time, will disrupt their flow."

"I think attempted murder can keep them occupied for a long while," Prisha added.

"Now, can we go back to the hotel?" Whitt asked, looking out the window into the darkness. "It's late, and my brain hurts."

"Yes, you may go home now. Thank you again for unraveling this morass," Evans replied.

"What time are you leaving tomorrow?" Finley asked Taylor.

"Around noon, after the first fishermen come in," Bobo replied instead. "While they're taking their noon meal, the waterways are less crowded. We can slip out then and take them to their boat."

"I will bring you back in the morning," Adesh said, as he and Bobo headed toward the door. "I'll wait outside for you."

Whitt, Prisha, and Taylor had stacked the dishes and headed into the kitchen. When Finley reached for Evans's bowl, he gently touched her arm.

"Thank you." He paused, as if uncertain whether to say more.

"You're welcome. We didn't do much of anything."

"You know as well as I that I would've died had you not come along."

"You're tougher than that," Finley said. "You could have lasted a couple more days until the next round of guests came in, or until the staff started making rounds."

"And they would've called the police, and the case would've been blown wide open. All that work gone. Lives lost for nothing."

"But it wasn't, and they didn't die without purpose."

"Yes, because of you and your sister," Evans said.

He laughed warily, mindful of his ribs. "I told you last time that sticking your nose in things was going to get you killed, but this time I am glad you didn't listen to me."

"You figured we wouldn't. Max has given up trying to get me to listen."

"How is Max?" Evans asked.

"He's fine," Finley said. "He's in Delhi."

"Is that where you are headed?" *The man doesn't mince words. Where he is going with this, I haven't a clue.*

"Yes. Does that surprise you?"

"No." Evans shook his head slowly, his hand still resting on her arm. "No. He's just a very lucky man."

The two were silent. Finley didn't know how to respond.

"And you?" Finley finally broke the quiet. "Where will you go to recuperate?"

"Probably Lyons. If they can get me that far," Evans said. "If not, maybe Mumbai. We'll see."

Whitt stuck her head in the room. She saw Evans's hand on Finley's arm and backed out.

"I'd better get this into the kitchen," Finley said. "You need to get some rest. You have a long trip ahead of you, wherever you end up."

"Thanks. See you tomorrow?" Evans's gaze asked more questions than the one he had mouthed.

Finley nodded, and bowl in hand, she walked out the door. Whitt met her in the kitchen.

"You ready to go or are you and Evans still talking?" she asked.

"I'm ready," Finley said. "Is everyone else outside?"

"Yeah. Bobo took Taylor to see where the boat could get into the lagoon. They just got back."

"Goodness, was I talking to Evans that long?" Finley asked.

"You were in there a pretty good stretch of time. Everything OK?" Whitt wanted to ask more, but she stopped herself. *That's her business. Not mine. She gave me space to figure out what I wanted. I owe her the same courtesy. I sure hope she knows what she's doing.*

Finley nodded and headed for the car.

Adesh met them in the drive outside the hotel the next morning. He had brought fresh bread from Lita, which Finley ran back and put into the room after stealing a pinch. They would eat the rest later, after Evans and the others had gone. After they said goodbye to Lita and the cousins. After things went back to normal.

"Is everyone up and ready?" Finley asked when she got back to the car.

"Yes, Lita has fed the whole crew. I picked up the others at the crack of dawn so they could prepare for their departure."

They drove the rest of the trip in silence. When they got to Lita's house, they found Evans, Taylor, and Prisha at the dining table. A map was laid out between them.

"We're trying to narrow down the places that the van Dijks might go," Prisha said.

"We put out an All Points for them. They'll have to surface at some point and with their pictures plastered all over, they will effectively be out of a job. Turpov won't like that so he may make a mistake that allows us to get him," Taylor added.

"They won't be too pleased with you," Whitt said. "Will they retaliate?"

"Probably, but not in the next few days," Evans said. "They'll have to find us first."

"You might want to stay 'dead' a little while longer," Finley said.

Evans laughed. "I might just do that. I could use a bit of vacation."

"We need to head out," Bobo said. "Your boat should be coming into position soon."

Lita passed Evans a small backpack. "In case it takes you a while to get to a doctor. Some pain meds and light wraps. You're going to feel the effects of travel before you reach your destination."

He gave her a hug before saying goodbye to Anu. He and Taylor got into the car with Bobo and waited until Finley, Whitt, and Prisha had thanked Adesh's family. When they reached the beach, Finley and Whitt could see a sailboat cresting the horizon.

Bobo quickly loaded Evans and his crew into the dinghy and headed to his boat. The plan was to use the larger vessel to rendezvous with their transport in open waters. Adesh and the sisters watched from shore as the crew climbed aboard Bobo's boat and entered the bay.

"What were you and Evans talking about so intently yesterday?" Whitt asked, her eyes locked on the boat as it met the horizon.

"Nothing much. Just life," Finley said, smiling. "He thinks Max is a lucky guy. Why, I haven't the slightest."

Whitt punched her sister's arm. "You had me worried. It looked like a pretty serious conversation."

"Well, you have no need to worry. Max and I are fine," Finley said with a dramatic comedic pause. "I think!"

The drive up the coast from Galle gave Finley and Whitt a last look at the varied topography that made Sri Lanka such a jewel. The lush green of the palms; the crystal blue of the waters; the sandy slivers of beach; the bright yellows, reds, and oranges of the fruit against the hills that rose gently from the sea before turning into mighty crags. This was indeed God's private paradise on earth.

Back in Colombo, Whitt wasted no time outlining her last-ditch shopping destinations—Plâté, Barefoot, and of course, Paradise Road. From having no interest in shopping at the beginning of the trip to full-out shopping frenzy by the end, Whitt managed to work through the shopping list that she had complied in record time. Finley and Whitt even managed to agree on a special thank you gift for Lita—a collage of photos Finley had snapped of Lita, Anu, Bobo, Adesh, and his other cousins, which she had had framed at Plâté.

"How you are going to get all of your stuff back—and where you're going to put it in your house—is beyond me," Finley said when the packages were laid out in the sitting room.

"I'm just going to Tbilisi, so if I get an extra bag, I should be fine," Whitt had clearly thought it all out.

Without David to carry all her purchases or to arrange their transport home, Whitt had resigned herself to just paying the weight overage. By the time the car came to take them to the airport, all the tsatskes had found a way home.

"Is Max really going to take the year off and travel with you?" Whitt had settled back in the seat for the ride through traffic.

"So he says. We'll see," Finley replied. "We have a few more months before he can wind his project down, so we have time to plan it out."

She continued, "But the real question is when are you and David getting married? Have you set a date? Have you even told Mama yet?"

"Yes and yes," Whitt said. "Mama is looking at options. Realistically, we're looking at next year. And that's just fine by me."

"I'll believe it when I see it," Finley joked. "You and Tbilisi Boy are just going to run off and jump the broom, and then tell Mama when it's a done deal."

Whitt recoiled in fake surprise. "Finley Walker Blake, I would never! But that doesn't mean I can't wish it were so."

She and Finley laughed at Mama's likely reaction. Apoplexy wouldn't be the half of it.

"Well, what about you and Max? You've been together longer than David and me."

Finley thought about what Whitt said. She and Max had indeed been together for almost three years, not counting the three-year separation that upended their lives and almost broke their hearts irreparably. She slowly twisted the Berber ring he had left for her when he had left for Delhi.

"Yeah, but we have time." *Endless time? Perhaps not. But endless love? Perhaps!*

The End

If you enjoyed this book and want to learn
more about Finley and Whitt Blake,
join our mailing list at www.mcarterfielding.com or
drop me a line at carter.fielding6554@gmail.com.
I'd love to hear from you.

Talk soon!

**Read on to get a sneak peek of the next adventure
in the Blake Sisters Travel Mystery Series**

ACKNOWLEDGMENTS

Every time I get to the last page of a book in the series, there is a bittersweetness that comes over me. A sense of both an ending and a new beginning since I know I will see these characters in the next installment of their saga. What I also know for sure is that as much as I thank those that have gotten me this far in my writing journey, I will see them again as we plan our next adventure with the Blake sisters.

- As always, I have to thank my mom and dad for allowing me the space to test out this new experiment with writing and for getting excited with me as I attack each new hurdle.
- The Guilted Sisters, as my cousins have taken to calling themselves, are another thank you that is in every book and will be until my pen is laid to rest. They got me into this and have been there at every turn to offer ideas, information, and insight. Like did you know that most Sri Lankan elephants, males included, don't have tusks?
- My book club has now also jumped in to add to my beta and advance reader base, offering me feedback both on the substance and the form of the books.

- In addition, I have found the power of mastermind groups in the creative and editing process. Thanks especially to Crys and J Thorn, who are never too busy with their own work to answer my whacky questions.
- Much appreciation also goes to the team and staff at Correspondance, a restaurant that I escape to once a week to write and edit.
- So much gratitude—and awe—goes to the Bublish team— Shilah, Kathy, and Eunice; my editor, whom I still only know by initials; the creative and tech team that make my messy drafts pretty; and all the others behind the scenes that keep me on track and headed toward publication.
- Finally, I offer my deep thanks to the growing base of readers that seem to be enjoying this crazy writing ride. Can't wait to get to know you better!

AUTHOR BIO

New author Carter Fielding is a millennial with an old soul. She likes old maps, old photographs, vintage records, and vintage champagnes. A Southerner, with roots in Anderson, South Carolina, she likes a good bourbon, a day that calls for wearing a barn jacket and a pair of wellies, and the smell of wet earth after a good rain. She started writing the Blake Sisters series during lockdown to tame a wanderlust that couldn't be satisfied by a trip to Harris Teeter and ended up building a relationship with the whole cast of characters that has taken on a life of its own.

She lives in Northern Virginia with her Boykin spaniel, Trucker, and uses her passion for books and travel to create characters she hopes readers will come to love.

CHAPTER 1

FINLEY **B**LAKE **WAS STANDING AT** the kitchen sink, watching her mother pace. She could see Mama talking to herself even as she continued the conversation with Finley's granny, whom Mama called Mom. *I am not going to let her guilt me. I am not going to let her guilt me.* Finley could see Mama's perfect, bow-shaped lips mouthing the words as her long legs swallowed up the length of the porch. Back and forth, back and forth. Clearly this conversation with Granny wasn't going as Mama had planned.

"Mom, I know we always come South for Thanksgiving and Christmas when we're in the States, but this year we need to be in St. Lucia." Mama looked out into the yard. She needed to ask Ry, her husband, to cut back the trailing vines that ran along the retaining wall before the snows of late December and January hit the mid-Atlantic. If not, the yard at their Chevy Chase house would be a jungle by spring.

Mama pushed back a strand of silken salt-and-pepper hair and lowered her voice. "Ry needs this. He needs this type of project if this design firm is going to work. This could be the break he needs, and I don't want to deny him that."

Granny, a tiny Southern hellcat in her eighties, must have had a counterargument to that, because Mama continued in a slow, steady voice: "Yes, I could bring the girls down alone, but I'm not going to do that. I'm going with my husband. To give what support I can. And yes, to enjoy some time in the sun."

Mama went on, "*Yes,* we'll come see you for Christmas. You know that. And that's only three weeks after we get back, so we'll be there in no time at all." Mama paused to let Granny grouse a little more. "Tell you what, even if Ry can't get away, as soon as Finley finishes her exams, we'll come down and stay until after New Year's. How does that sound?"

Mama was moving into appeasement mode. That normally got Finley's granny to cease the frontal attack and prepare for the flanking maneuvers that would start as soon as Mama hung up the phone. Granny would call Aunt Julie and then Aunt Peggy, Mama's sisters. Aunt Julie would start on how sick their mom has been and what a shock to her system this change in plans would cause. When that failed to soften Mama up, they would sic Aunt Peggy on her with her balancing act.

"I understand how torn you must be. Wanting to support Ry. He is your husband, after all. But you know how important the holidays are to Mom. She likes having us all together, especially now that you don't have to travel like you did when Ry was in the service." Aunt Peggy would emphasize the *have,* as if to suggest that even then there had been a choice that Mama had refused to make.

Aunt Peggy would then deliver the coup de grâce. "We don't know how many more holidays we're going to have with her." She would pause for effect before picking up again in her easy, singsong drawl. "So, we have to take advantage of all the ones we have."

From the look on Mama's face, she was steeling herself for the barrage of arguments that was to come. She had put the phone on the table after hanging up with her mother and sat looking at it, daring it to ring. When it did, she was ready.

"Hey. Yes, I did just talk to Mom. Nope, she didn't make it up. Yeah, it's too bad, but it can't be helped this time." Mama was keeping her voice neutral, light even, but the little crease between her brow told another story. Finley was tempted to tease her and tell her to relax her face or it would freeze like that—something she was always telling Finley and Whitt, her younger sister. But now didn't seem like the right time.

Finley was glad her daddy wasn't around to overhear the conversation. Daddy was a gentle giant of a man who held his temper, except when it was needed to protect one of his girls. And Mama was his main girl. He would not take kindly to the browbeating going on now.

Finley couldn't tell from the conversation whether it was Aunt Peggy or Aunt Julie on the phone. Mama was laying down the law, whoever it was.

"I respect your concern for Mom, and I respect her desire to have family with her at Thanksgiving. But it isn't going to happen this year. And don't start with that cock-and-bull crap about her not being around for next year. *I* may be dead, but that old bird will still be clucking. So please save Julie the effort and relay the message that we will see you all at Christmas. Love you." With that, she clicked off her phone and sat staring at its screen until a picture of the four of them at Finley's college graduation came up.

"I know you're there and heard all of it. There will be no more discussion about it. Nary a mention to your daddy. Is that understood?" She turned and looked at Finley, who stood in the doorway holding her Crim Law textbook in her hands.

"Yes, ma'am," Finley answered. She hesitated before asking, "You all right?"

Had it been Daddy, she would have gone and hugged away the hurt, but Mama and Whitt could be prickly, so she approached them like she would an injured cat, careful of the claws. Today, they were retracted.

"Yes, baby, I'm fine," Mama sighed. "Sorry you had to hear that, but that is my reality."

She chuckled and signaled Finley over. Finley approached and planted a kiss on her mother's forehead.

"We'll have a good time, Mama. You know we will. So just put all that madness out of your head."

The flight to St. Lucia took longer than the distance on the map suggested it would. Daddy said he could have almost swum the distance faster. Mama just shook her head and went back to her magazine. During most of the flight, Finley had her head stuck in her law books, trying to finish as much of her required reading as she could so that she could spend at least some time on the beach or in the water.

She liked law school—the rigor of the studying and those eureka moments when muddled musings suddenly made sense. She wasn't sure, however, that she liked the law. Her sense of justice was often affronted by outcomes of cases that rang true based on the logic of precedence, but fell short of what she thought was right. She knew it might disappoint her parents, who were especially proud to have a budding lawyer in the family, but she didn't think she would ever want to practice.

She wondered, given that, why she was working so hard to make the law journal. She realized her unmistakable truth. She hated to lose. She refused to fold just because she thought she might lose. She was driven to find a way to play the hand she was given with the hope that she would win. Thus far, she was still in the game.

"So, what do you want to do while we're there?" Whitt, her baby sister by almost six years, was sitting in the window seat beside her, perusing the pages of a guidebook she had found that outlined the activities at the resort, as well as other worthwhile sights on the island. "They say here that there are loads of little shops with handicrafts that we should check out when we aren't on the beach."

"I want to try kayaking," Finley declared. "And maybe some swimming. I'm going to have to fit that in between studying. I still have a lot of reading to do. But nobody said I couldn't read in my bathing suit!"

The car from Anse Annette met them outside the baggage claim. Charles, a broad-shouldered, sepia-brown man with eyes

that smiled, peeked around the bib of his porkpie hat and introduced himself as their driver. They were the only passengers in the
Land Rover.

"You are it for now. A few other guests are getting in tonight. A
couple of people arrived last week. We have a famous French movie
star staying with us. Nathalie Lavail. You may have heard of her?"
Charles asked Mama, who nodded.

Charles continued, "She has been here for about a week. She
comes at least twice a year and stays in the bungalow." He lowered
his voice to a stage whisper before breaking into a belly laugh. "She
likes her privacy."

The road from Soufrière, the nearest town, was steep and rocky,
and the brown and gray of the rugged track contrasted sharply
with the soft, leafy canopy of green that surrounded them as they
turned away from the sea and into the hills. As they bumped along,
Finley understood why the hotel used Land Rovers instead of vans
for transport. She feared that she would get whiplash from all the
jolting or that a bag would come hurtling over the backseat and
crash into her head. Charles, all the while, seemed not to notice
the rugged terrain. He kept asking Daddy what brought him to
St. Lucia and then about the condo project. In between, he filled
in Whitt and Finley on all the water sports that were available on
the property.

"This is a diver's paradise, our little cove. The fish are so many
and so colorful." Charles turned to look at Finley, "Do you dive?
Training is included in the package if you don't."

"I snorkel, but I've never tried diving," Finley replied. "Maybe
I'll give it a try."

"Are there other hotels around? This seems awfully isolated,"
Daddy asked, searching out the windows for signs of life amid the
steeply banked jungle on either side of the road.

"There are a few other hotels on this part of the island, but you
can really only see them from the sea," Charles responded. "You will

find that besides arrivals and departures, which are by road, we do everything else by sea. Hope you don't get seasick!"

He laughed to himself as they bumped and jostled along the rocky road toward the hotel. After twenty minutes or so, the road veered to the left and down a steeply graded incline before ending in a large, circular drive that fronted the main entrance to the hotel. While a bellman transferred the luggage from the back of the SUV into a small, three-wheeled truck with oversized tank treads, Charles described the layout of the resort.

"You will be staying at one of our hillside villas. There are eighteen of them, and six of the smaller beach cabanas. And then there is the bungalow that Miss Nathalie stays in and the maxi-villa at the top that the Prescotts are in," Charles explained as he pointed to the amenities on the property. "We are kind of in the middle of the string of rooms now. You take that path to the beach, that one to the dive shop, and that one there to the jungle and the ruins. We have over 600 acres, so you'll never get bored."

He turned to shake hands with each of them before getting back in the Land Rover and heading further down the hill. A lady in a turquoise madras dress and headscarf came out carrying a tray of drinks to greet them.

"Welcome to Anse Annette! While we see to your room, please come and enjoy the view."

She led them past the front desk and small, art-gallery shop into a large, octagonal room with a raffia ceiling and wooden-lattice railing. The room opened up to a view of the sea, offering breathtaking scenery. The building where the reception area was housed was suspended above a layer of lush green canopy that stretched into a broad streak of aqua-blue water, deepening into indigo as the bay moved to the ocean.

Mama and Daddy stopped, slack-jawed, in the middle of the room.

"This is heaven on earth, Ry. My goodness, I may never leave!"

"Many of our guests say that. And we are glad for you to stay forever!" the young receptionist shared. "But for now, please sit and rest while we prepare your keys."

She showed them to a cluster of bent cane chairs and low wooden tables along the railing. Another young woman in pink madras, the national fabric with its bright-colored tartan weave, came around with cool, sweetly scented towels that she pulled from a round, woven basket. Once she had collected the towels, the receptionist placed drinks in front of them.

"We will be with you shortly," she said before heading toward the front desk.

"This is good!" Mama was trying to isolate the flavors in the concoction that they were drinking. Her culinary training had kicked in, and she was working on discerning the spices, having already nailed down the juices that were in it. "A bit of cinnamon, nutmeg, and I think there is some mace in there, as well. And a touch of cardamom."

"I'm impressed. All I tasted was juice!" Daddy teased. "Now, if there'd been something stronger in it, I don't think I'd have had any problem finding all the notes and nuances."

Mama gave him a playful shove and shook her finger at him. "Don't you go making fun of me!"

Finley and Whitt looked at their parents bantering and giggled. They knew that the next step in this love dance that their parents played was Daddy taking Mama's hand and telling her how much he loved her and how lucky he was to get to call her his girl. They sipped on their drinks, glancing out at the water, and waited. As if on cue, Daddy reached for Mama's hand. Just as he did, the receptionist returned.

"I will show you to your villa now." She led the way to the path.

"You can tell her later how much you love her," Whitt whispered when she drew alongside her father. He feigned mock surprise and then winked in agreement, quickening his pace to catch up with his wife. He casually slipped her hand in his as they mounted the stairs to their villa on the hillside.

"I bet that climb will make you girls remember to take everything with you to the beach when you go down—or do without!" Mama warned them when they reached the door to their villa. It had been quite a trudge. The lady, who had said her name was Harriet, mentioned something about there being close to one hundred steps between the clubhouse and the two upper villas, of which this was one.

"Let me show you around." Harriet opened the door and stood aside for them to enter. They had gotten no more than ten steps into the room before they all stopped again. If the view from the clubhouse reception area had been spectacular, the panorama now was otherworldly.

Above the trees, almost above the clouds, the living area was open on three sides, allowing a wide-angle view of the bay and parts of the expanse of ocean. To the far left loomed the majestic Pitons, the twin mountains that had dominion over the southwestern part of the island, seemingly close enough to be touched. Small boats painted in combinations of blues, reds, and oranges crept into the bay and crept out, barely leaving a trace on the blue-ink gloss of the water.

"They call what we just walked up the 'Stairway to Heaven.' I think you can see why." Harriet unlocked the door. "The villa at the top is larger and has a pool, but I personally like the way this one is positioned to take advantage of both the sea and the mountains."

The villa rested on a shelf cut into the hill. The first floor was dominated by the living area, which was divided into a large, central sitting area with two facing sofas and a couple of chairs in bright madras prints arranged around a large, wooden coffee table, a dining area large enough to seat eight, and a smaller reading or conversation nook along one side of the terrace. Along the back of the room was a bright-green kitchenette with a mini-fridge, a microwave, and a sink.

Upstairs, there were two bedrooms, each with en suite bathrooms, and between them, another sitting area with a small library. All three rooms, decked out in vibrant madras variants of pinks, blues, and greens, were open to vistas of the sea and cooled by the mountain air. Mama and Daddy's room was the largest and had louvered shutters that opened to expose a palette of blues that were shared by the bay, the ocean, and the cloudless sky. Another tropical-print sofa, a wooden coffee table, a café table, and some rattan, barrel lounge chairs occupied the space—and there was still left room for a tango or two.

"There's a swing, Mama!" Whitt cried when they got to the sisters' room. "There's a big old swing!"

The wooden garden swing, large enough to seat two, was hung in the bedroom at an angle that caught the sunset over the bay. Whitt and her sister claimed their rightful places in the swing and pushed off. Whitt's grin and Finley's smile said all that was needed about whether they liked their room.

It didn't take long for the sisters to unpack and claim their respective sides of the bed. Whitt was so excited about getting to the beach that she actually beat Finley in the race to get changed and pack her things—a rarity almost equal to the spotting of Halley's Comet.

"Can we go down to the beach now, Mama?" Whitt stood at the door to her parents' room. "We're all unpacked."

Mama looked to Finley for confirmation. Finley nodded.

"Then go on down. There are beach towels in the hall closet. Grab a couple for us and use them to save Daddy and me lounge chairs. We'll be down in a bit."

Whitt shot out the door so quickly she almost bowled over the lanky young man walking down the stairs in front of the villa. A young girl and a younger boy who were following him gasped at the near run-in.

"Sorry. I wasn't expecting anyone else to be around," Whitt apologized.

"No harm, no foul." The young man sized up the two young women in their beach cover-ups and smiled. "You guys must have just checked in. I'm Noah. That's Lucy and Ian, my sibs." He pointed to a girl around twelve and a boy about ten.

"I'm Whitt, and this is my sister, Finley."

"Where're you guys from?" The boy had started down the stairs, and the rest of the group followed. He paused until Whitt was next to him before he continued down the steep incline.

"Washington, DC. Just outside," she answered.

Whitt looked over at him as he walked with his head down beside her. He and his siblings were some of the blondest people Whitt had ever seen. Their hair, as well as of their eyebrows, was almost bleached out, offering a nice counterpoint to their tanned skin. They looked like straight-out-of-a-magazine Californians to her, so she was surprised when he responded, "New York, the city," to her same question about hometown.

When they reached the end of the path, the beach was almost empty. Finley headed over to some chairs a fair distance from the walkway while Noah and his siblings wandered over to a space closer to the dive shop. Whitt followed her new friends. She figured that her sister wouldn't mind. Finley was going to study anyway, whether Whitt was there or not. When she looked over at her sister, she saw that she was right. Finley had stripped off her cover-up but sat upright with a textbook in her lap, her alligator-green eyes fixed on the text.

"What's your sister studying so hard?" Noah asked, glancing over at Finley. "She has her SATs or something coming up?"

Whitt laughed. *He thinks Finley is still in high school. I guess she doesn't look that old, but she doesn't look that young, either. I wonder how old he thinks I am.*

"No, she's in law school. She has to keep up with her reading." Whitt pulled off her cover-up and headed toward the water as she spoke. Noah seemed to be processing the information.

She was so mesmerized by the warmth of the water that she didn't catch Noah running his eyes over her long, shapely form before she dove in. While she didn't have Finley's natural curves, she was toned, with a thin, athletic build. Something Noah seemed to appreciate. He joined her as she swam out a bit from the shore, treading water as she looked back to the beach.

"Who's that?" Whitt's attention was drawn to two people whose upper torsos were visible on the terrace of the house that was behind Finley. It was a man and a woman, but she couldn't make out much more than that.

"Some French film star who was famous a long time ago. She's pretty old. The guy she's with is a lot younger. I mean, a *heck* of a lot younger," Noah smirked for some reason that Whitt couldn't figure.

Between the quick swims that they took in the clear blue water, she listened to him talk about himself—a lot about himself. When she wasn't underwater or distracted by the apparent argument between the film star and her friend, she heard him say that he was eighteen, a freshman at Hobart, a college she had heard of but one that wasn't on her list of potentials, and likely to follow his father into investment banking, about which Whitt was clueless. She kept her answers about herself short so that she didn't seem too juvenile. *He is so cute. And in college, no less. Please, don't let me sound like a dweeb.*

It wasn't until they discovered their mutual interest in horses that her hesitation dissipated, and the conversation flowed like spring water. It turned out that he had been riding since he was nine; she since she was five. He was an eventer; she showed as a hunter. By the time Mama and Daddy came down, they had reviewed their equestrian histories and made tentative plans for a ride during their stay.

"Whitt, you need to come on in and get dressed for dinner," Mama called from the beach after a while.

When Whitt and Noah reached shore, Daddy and Mama were talking to two human beanpoles who were as tow-headed as their children. Noah introduced his parents to Whitt as Jonathan and Kris Prescott. He quickly shook hands with Mama and Daddy before waving goodbye and heading off toward his siblings. *He clearly doesn't like the company of adults, or maybe it's just his parents he was running away from. They seem nice enough. Strange. I hope Mama didn't think he was rude. I'll never hear the end of it.*